THE BLOOD OF BIGFOOT

A NOVEL BY MICHAEL COLE

SEVERED PRESS
HOBART TASMANIA

THE BLOOD OF BIGFOOT

WWW.SEVEREDPRESS.COM

ISBN: 978-1-922323-85-9

CHAPTER 1

The beast awoke.

For fifty years, it felt nothing but the subtle heartbeat in its chest. During hibernation, most organisms maintained a heartrate of twenty-beats per minute. The humanoid beast only needed ten. When its heart struck its 13,140,000th beat, its body shifted like a dormant volcano coming to life. Its heartrate climbed to fifty-per-minute, pushing its bloodstream like a hellish lava flow.

Its eyes opened. It had not dreamt, as its body did not produce the electric currents necessary during hibernation. In those decades, its brain was powered down, sending only the signals necessary for its body to perform the basic functions of survival.

It sat up and took in the dark underground world around it. There was nothing to see, as there was no sunlight. It relied on memory to visualize its habitat. The next step was to breathe. A deep inhale brought the smell of dirt into its nostrils. Within that smell was also that of urine and feces, but most had been lost to decay during the years. Its claws curled by its legs, feeling the hardened soil underneath it. It was all the same, other than the scent of additional rot. Other than that, it was as if the creature had lain itself to rest yesterday.

There was no cognizance of the passage of time other than the weakness it felt. Its body had burnt through its fat reserves during its hibernation. When it buried itself, its midsection was rounded with fat from endless eating. Now, its figure was lean, its arms and legs stiff.

The hunger called to it like a demonic voice. It was time to perform the first ritual of life. The creature stood up, its head grazing the dirt roof. Its knees popped, as did its elbows and knuckles. It stretched once, loosening its joints. The hunger called again, this time triggering a pain in its abdomen. It needed sustenance to convert to fat. If the beast found nothing, its muscular structure would be the next thing to dissolve.

It felt around the walls and found the mouth of the lair. It was slanted, full of rotted roots and rocks. Sticking an arm's length out of the wall were three tree branches, smoothened and spaced from the center. The beast had done this intentionally to assist with the process of digging out. But despite that, the task required effort and time. Afterall, it was more than a simple action; freeing itself was a test of strength—a reawakening of the body.

Its hand found a branch sticking out of the wall like a doorknob. It wrapped its fingers around the edge and pulled. Its body shook with the struggle. The branch didn't budge. The dirt wall had hardened in the time spent sleeping, securing the branches in place. *This* was the test of strength. It pulled again. The branch nudged a bit, but still remained in place.

The third tug brought bits of dried earth crumbling down. Hungry and frustrated, the beast struck the wall, as it did with every awakening. Its fist struck like a hammer, loosening the dirt's firm hold. Its strength was building. Its heartbeat rose, pushing its blood like river rapids. Its senses were heightened. Its oxygen supply had been used up. Its stomach was roaring like a beast from an era older than itself. Desperation spurred its resolve.

It grabbed the branch with both hands, stomped its enormous foot against the dirt, and pulled with all its might. The branch shook and cracked. The beast did not let up. Its arms continued rearing back, twitching from resistance, but slowly succeeding in their task.

The branch came free, bringing with it a huge mound of dirt out of the wall. Incited by hunger and its progress towards satisfying it, the creature found the next branch. It only took one mighty pull to free this one, as the wall around it was weakened. When the beast freed the third branch, the wall crumbled into a loose mound of soil.

Like a moth emerging from its cocoon, the creature clawed at the dirt wall. Handfuls of sediment splattered the cave floor behind it. Like wading through deep water, the creature pushed through. Its arms were like oars steering a massive ship against an icy current.

Dirt fell all around it. Then, it took in the scent of clean air. It followed the path on its upward slant, until it felt the final layer of hardened mud. Grassroots dangled above its nose.

Its fist ruptured the earth's surface with a burst of dirt and grass. Squeezing its other hand through the newly created gap, it pulled the earthy 'door' to its lair apart. Sunlight embraced its face. Smells, new, yet familiar, made their way to its brain. It saw pine green trees around it, some larger than when it went down.

The creature emerged into the world and shook the dirt from its fur. It was free. There was no time for curious wandering, as it didn't care about the advances in the world around it. All it cared about was the taste of meat and the gratifying feeling of snapping bones. Only the strong survived in nature, and *it* was the strongest.

It stomped its mighty foot into the earth and roared. Its new rein had begun.

CHAPTER 2

"Should we move now?"

Robert Windle sighed. His cousin had grown increasingly restless in the last couple of hours. For five hours they waited in the same spot with a semi-clear field of view, and yet, not a single deer had wandered in their vicinity.

Oak Grave Forest was displaying signs of the autumn season. The leaves on the elm, sugar maple, and red oak trees were taking on their red and brown colors. The grass wasn't quite as green as in the summer, and much of it was covered in dead leaves that coiled like dead insect husks.

Small critters scurried about, packing their underground layers with acorns and other resources provided by the forest. There were still a few birds overhead, but the population had decreased to about a third, as the rest had begun flying south.

It seemed like they saw every living thing in this forest except the one they were after.

A cool breeze hit Robert's face. The temperature had dropped to fifty degrees. Not freezing, but just cold enough where he wasn't comfortable without his coffee. Unfortunately, his thermos was empty, as was Jake's. He checked his watch and saw that it was a quarter after six. Considering the poor luck they were having, perhaps it was time to call it a day. There was always tomorrow.

Still, there was a greedy competitiveness that prevented Robert from throwing in the towel. When he arrived in Oak Grave yesterday, he and Jake ran into an old college friend, Lou Judd. They had hunted together a lot in their early twenties, and Robert always managed to show him up by either being the only one to shoot a deer, or by bringing home the biggest one. He had what many hunters lacked: patience. He knew that if he waited long enough, those six-point antlers would eventually emerge from behind the trees.

Had he not seen Lou, he would've had the good decency to call it a day. Worse yet; had he not heard the distant cracks of Lou's .30-30, he would call it a day. No way in hell was Robert willing to let Lou show him up. Even now, being in his mid-thirties, his ego had never wavered.

"It's getting cold," Jake complained again. He pulled his hat down over his ears, only for his thick bushy brown hair to push it back up.

"Stop being such a pussy," Robert hissed.

"Speaking of which, I need to piss."

Robert glanced at him. It took him a second to put two-and-two together.

"No, I didn't say 'pissy', I said stop being a *pussy*."

"I need that too," Jake muttered. "Not as much as you though, with how cranky you've been lately." He slowly emerged from the log they were crouched behind, leaving his shotgun resting against it as he stepped behind a tree. Robert kept his eyes on the patch of forest in front of them, while trying to tune out the sound of Jake's zipper and the stream hitting the dead leaves.

Robert grimaced. Jake HAD to mention that. Yeah, it was a passive way of stating it, but he knew what he was getting at. Still, he couldn't help but feel his left ring finger under his glove. Six months ago, he thought he'd feel the tightness of a ring on it by this time.

What is it with Jake waiting until I'm already in a foul mood to bring shit like this up?

No wonder he wanted a deer. This year sucked, so far. His sports retail business was failing, his engagement had abruptly ended; a month ago, his truck broke down.

All I want is a buck. Is that too much to ask?

Probably so, with how loudly his cousin was urinating. If anything was nearby, it certainly would've been scared off by now. Still, the thought of heading back to the cabin wasn't appealing. All he would do was fixate on his misery. At least here, he was distracted by the mesmerizing experience of being in tune with nature. No, he wasn't ready to go yet. He didn't care how bored Jake was.

"Alright, let's go a little further," Robert declared. Jake zipped himself up, then looked to the sky in misery. His mind cycled through a few arguments, but realized none of them would have any effect on Robert. Except—maybe the 'dinner' argument.

"Aren't you hungry?" Jake said.

"I brought a couple Nutri-Grain bars," Robert replied. Jake made a 'blech' sound. He was an average built man, certainly not overweight by any means, but he wanted REAL food—not this wholegrain shit that Robert was in to. To the guy's credit, though, he did drop about ten pounds of fat and replace it with ten pounds of muscle. If he had anything going for him this year, it was physical fitness and health.

They stepped over the log and slowly pressed west into the forest. After a few minutes of walking, Robert could see a clearing up ahead. They were nearing the Spruce Trail.

Hmm. Maybe we'll have better luck if we keep going this way.

"We could head northwest and try by the lake," Jake said. Robert thought about it for a moment. It wasn't a terrible idea, though he was surprised Robert would suggest a mile-long walk. Perhaps he had resigned himself to another couple of hours of hunting. Also, following the trail would be an easier trek than walking through the woods.

Even so, there was the natural instinct to say no and keep going east. Not that he didn't agree with Jake, but his superiority complex sparked a desire to always be the one with the best ideas. However, going with Jake's suggestion would likely spare him from listening to another hour or so of complaining.

"Alright," Robert said. *Hopefully we don't pass any game on the way there.*

"Should we take the ATV?"

Robert looked back at the four-wheeler that came with the cabin rental.

"No. Don't want to scare off anything I oughta be shooting," he replied. "We'll keep up with the walk and if we find anything, we'll hike back up here and brink it to the kill."

Jake sighed, rocking his aching feet. Resigned to his cousin's wishes, he followed Robert to the trail. They turned north. The reflection of sunlight struck his face, making him squint. It was another one of those memorial plaques.

In memory of Joseph Wheeler and Audrey Edwards.

This plaque was newer and practically made out of pure gold! The other ones were carved in stone or inscribed in wooden benches along the various trails in the forest.

God, you'd think these kids were U.S. Presidents with the number of memorials they've gotten, Robert thought.

Jake always shuddered whenever he saw the plaques. Somewhere in the back of his mind, whenever he hunted in Oak Grove Forest, he secretly feared he'd stumble across the rotted skeletons of the two teenagers who went missing back in 1970. While bored one day, he read up on the incident on the internet. Joseph and Audrey were recent High School graduates who had just gotten engaged. Accounts from Audrey's family indicated they loved wandering through the forest. Then, in the late summer of 1970, they wandered into the woods together and never returned.

That's when the story got even more interesting. During the search, one of the deputies and his rescue dog mysteriously vanished. No radio call. No gunshots. The man just vanished as though swallowed by the forest. For the next decade, hardly anyone ventured into the forest.

But time heals all wounds and quells most fears, and eventually, things returned to normal. The deer population had exploded and life resumed. The trails were paved, the Beasley couple had purchased a speck of land, on which they built their ranch. In the fifty-years between 1970 and 2020, there wasn't a single reported incident. Whoever had abducted the teens and deputy was long gone.

"Check this out," Robert said. Jake snapped out of his trance and looked to the left. His cousin took a few steps into the woods and knelt down. When he returned, he had a chewed cigar stub between his fingers, with a blue label that read *Royal Ayres Cigars*. Robert snickered. "Lou's been out this way."

In the decade-and-a-half that they'd known Lou Judd, he was always smoking that brand of cigar. Very rarely did the guy try something new, and that was with all of life. He hunted in the same woods, used the same rifle, lived in the same house, drove the same truck—which Robert resented since his wasn't as old, yet broke down on him, while Lou's ran just fine despite having nearly two-hundred-thousand miles on it.

Jake could read his cousin's mind. *If Lou found something out this way, maybe we can too.* He looked at his watch again. Six-thirty. They were only a week away from daylight savings, and sky was already showing hints of dusk.

"I'll stick with you for another hour, then I'm heading in. No way am I wandering out here after dark," he said.

"Fine. Then make sure you keep up," Robert replied. He turned left and wandered through the tree line.

"I thought we were walking the trail," Jake exclaimed.

"Dude, we've been doing this *how many years*?" Robert replied. "We'll keep close to the trail, but we're not walking ON it. God only knows what we'll pass. Come on, quit wasting time." With a subdued groan, Jake followed his cousin through the uneven terrain covered in exposed roots, dirt mounds, and the remnants of dead trees. All the way through, his mind played tricks on him, envisioning the white-grey bones and slack jaws of human skeletons laying in every corner. "And stop being such a pussy," Robert said again, looking at his nervous expression. "Jesus, you're worse than my five-year-old nephew going into a haunted house."

****

Another cool breeze swept over the hunters as they continued north on foot. This one was colder, as it was coming off the lake which resided in the center of the twenty-three square miles of forest. Jake's knees were starting to ache, first from sitting for so long, and now from moving through these seemingly untamed woods.

He moved to the left to get around a tree, only to practically walk face-first right into a bush. He felt the wet, yet sticky sensation of a spider web clinging to his unshaven face. On that silky mess was the spider that weaved it, coiling its forelegs inches from his right eye. Up close, the arachnid looked like something from his worst nightmares.

"Jesus! Jesus! Jesus! Fuck! Fuck! Fuck! Get off!"

Robert turned around and watched as Jake clawed at his face, peeling away at the arachnid and the web. He stopped for a moment, only to see the thing now on his glove. Jake shrieked again, unstrapped the glove, and threw it deep into the woods.

Jake's hair bounced in thick coils as he tore off his hat and checked it for webbing. His eyes then went to his cousin, who watched with that disapproving stare he constantly wore.

"What?"

"Congratulations, dipshit. Everything for miles heard you," Robert said. Jake took a moment before responding, as he wasn't sure if Robert was being sarcastic, or was genuinely irritated. Judging by that narrow gaze, it was the latter.

Now, Jake was getting pissed.

"Give me a break, man," he spoke loudly...and purposely, which provoked the desired expression in Robert's face. *Yeah-yeah, act like you're God's gift to mankind. Can't say I can't understand why Christine left you.* "I'm starving. My legs are killing me. I just wanna head in, have a burger, and beer...something I think you could use as well."

To his surprise, Robert did not get pissed at that statement. Maybe his body was finally alerting him to the fact that he hadn't eaten anything but Nutria-Grain bars for the last seven hours. Still, there was a part of him that didn't want to admit defeat. Plus, going in was Jake's idea, and that superiority complex was demanding he be the one to decide when they left.

"Go find your glove," he said.

Jake waved his hand at him then trekked into the woods where he tossed the item. Patrick Windle was always hot-and-cold to be around, and it always depended on his mood. He wasn't the most particularly well-liked during family reunions or Thanksgiving dinners, *especially* when he hosted.

"Christ, why do I do this to myself?" he muttered. He shuffled through some of the bushes in search of the brown-and-orange glove. He was losing daylight fast. Part of him considered cutting his losses and turning back. Then again, this pair of gloves were a gift from his sister, who'd be pissed if she found out he willfully left it in the woods.

Okay, I tossed it this direction…

He bent back the branches of a bush but saw no signs of the item. A fly buzzed by his head. He smacked at it, then groaned. It was late October, and the bastards were still buzzing. He'd hardly seen any bugs all day, yet all of a sudden it was as though the season had turned to spring. He could hear the buzzing of wings all around him. Again, he swatted.

"Damn bugs. You'd think the fifty-degrees would send y'all undergr—ah, finally!" He found his glove tilted along a tree root. He hurried to it, snatched it up, then started to turn around. Another breeze swept through the woods. A horrible odor filled his nose. Jake Cobb had hunted long enough to know the smell of blood and rotting flesh. It was the forest, after all. In the forest, there were animals, alive and dead.

However, it wasn't the smell that locked his vision to the north. Even when the next breeze assaulted his eyes, he didn't even blink.

Is it just me, or is that tree actually covered in blood?

It was thirty feet away, partially obscured by the branches of a pine and elm tree that stood in-between it and Jake. He took a few steps toward it. As if it had a mind of its own, the shotgun was shouldered, pointed slightly lower. His finger rested against the trigger guard, ready to find its way home. His heart skipped a beat when he passed between the trees and the ferns in-between them.

The ground was like the surface of Mars, only darker—more brown than red. Perhaps hell was a better description, which his mind settled on after seeing the protruding rib bones. He wasn't sure what he was looking at initially. It was just a heap of flesh lying on the ground with no distinct shape, like a bloodied potato sack.

He heard snapping twigs behind him.

"Jesus, Jake, you find a date over here or something?" Robert said. His cousin didn't offer a response. Robert followed his gaze into the woods, then saw the blood and the bones. "What the—" He readied his rifle and cautiously approached.

Intestines and organs were coiled along the ground, covered by swarms of ants. The fur, what little was left, was brown in color. The body was ripped across the center, exposing much of the ribcage and spinal column. There was no head or limbs…at least, not attached to the body.

"It's a deer," Robert said.

"How do you know?" Jake asked. Robert swallowed, then pointed a few meters past the carcass. At first, Jake thought he was pointing at a broken branch, then realized he was looking at a pair of antlers.

The two men slowly approached. Jake felt something long and narrow roll under his boot. He looked down, then gasped. Robert grabbed him by the shoulder to keep him from bumping into him. Before he could chastise his cousin again, Robert looked down at where Jake stepped. They had found one of the deer's legs. It was fully intact, aside from the fact that it had been torn out by the roots.

He glanced around. Somewhere in the surrounding brush were the other three legs. The deer had been literally drawn and quartered, as though sentenced to death in some medieval kingdom.

"Something had a good time," Robert said.

"*What?*" Jake asked, nervously peering in every direction, then back at the corpse. It had literally been pulled apart, including the ribcage. Its insides were mostly gone. He looked over at the head. Its eyes had been gouged, the snout bent into a fishhook shape.

"Bear perhaps," Robert said, unconvincingly.

"No bear does shit like this," Jake said. "Must be some psycho in these woods."

"He'd have to be built like *Dwayne Johnson,* AND be high on meth," Robert replied. He looked to the north. "Whatever it is, it went that way."

Up ahead were a series of crushed bushes and broken branches. The leaves attached were only partially dry, meaning the branch had been broken for maybe half a day. He looked at the broken end of the limb. It was two-inches thick, and broken off with hardly any fraying at the end. Whatever had done this broke it off in a single snap. A human would have to have Olympian strength to break it so cleanly.

That's when he noticed something else; a rounded crater in the trunk of the tree. A .30.06. It was high, at least seven feet up. Who shot this, and what the hell were they shooting at?

"Wait a sec..."

Robert turned around and inspected the ravaged neck of the deer. He grabbed the antlers and tilted the head away from him. Not far from the stump was a single bullet wound.

"Someone shot this deer and tracked it..." he said. He stood straight and ventured into the trail of ravaged vegetation. Twigs snapped beneath his boots. The dried leaves had covered the earth, obscuring any tracks. Some of the elm and maple trees were already barren on this end of the forest.

His eyes panned to the left. Standing out from all the brown and red leaves was a blue speck. He walked over to it, knelt down, and brushed away some of the leaves. He saw the pitchfork logo and the words *Royal Ayres Cigars.* The stogie it was attached to was only half-smoked.

Lou Judd had been here.

The hairs on the back of Robert's neck were starting to stand. Lou used a 30.06...and he *never* wasted cigars. He shuffled through some of the leaves for any more clues.

Jake had beaten him to it.

"Psst!"

He was making an effort to be quiet, which set Robert even more on edge. He stood up slowly and looked to his right. Jake was peeking behind a thick tree, then turned back. His face had paled. With clenched teeth, he rested with his back to the tree. He looked over at Robert, then cocked his head back to whatever was on the other side.

You look.

Robert gripped his rifle tight, then approached. Jake remained leaning back against the tree like a soldier taking cover from enemy fire, gladly willing to let his cousin take the assault instead. Robert placed one foot ahead of the other, climbed the small mound leading to the base of the tree, then peeked. There was nothing there. Not alive, anyway. Just an ocean of dried blood.

It was everywhere, as though the victim had been hung from a branch and opened like a jug.

Robert took a breath and pushed on. Now, he was glancing at the surrounding forest. He didn't know what he was searching for, but he knew they weren't alone out here.

His gaze moved back to the dried puddle. There was something in the middle—some sort of mass.

"What is it? Is it a man?" Jake whispered. Robert held up a hand, signaling for him to wait. It didn't make a difference—Jake was still behind the tree. Robert stood over the thing but couldn't bring himself to touch it.

Gently, he prodded it with the muzzle of his rifle. The thing folded inward like an empty husk. It was fabric. A jacket! When he brushed the leaves off of it, the features became obvious. It was unzipped, the inner fabric also caked with blood. It peeled apart when he pulled the corner of it, stretching red gooey strands. Robert wheezed, then staggered back.

His heel hit something under a few leaves. Another tree limb? No, this had a smoother surface. He looked down and saw the bent barrel of a Browning 30.06 rifle. The bolt action had been pulled back, the muzzle crumpled and hooked under the barrel.

On the frame were the initials *L.J.*

It took several minutes for both men to track far enough back up the trail to get a phone signal.

Robert held it high until finally he got a bar. For the dozenth time, he tried calling 9-1-1. Finally, someone answered.

"Yes. My name's Robert Windle, calling from the Spruce Trail in Oak Grove Forest. We need the police here immediately. I think there's been a murder."

CHAPTER 3

When the call came in, Chief Walter Eastman's shirt was unbuttoned and half untucked, ready to be yanked off when he got in his pickup. He usually stayed a few hours later on Friday nights, particularly during the hunting season. Usually by this time, everyone had come in, aside from a few people who enjoyed some late night fishing at the lake. Even though the trails officially closed at 8:30, he never bothered sending his officers to check them out. As long as the Beasleys or cabin tenants didn't complain, what were people really hurting by being out there so late? The trails themselves were straightforward, so there was almost no chance of people getting lost.

Walter shrunk in his office chair when the word 'murder' entered his eardrums. Not that he was unfamiliar with handling violent crime scenes, but because he was *too* familiar. Twenty-years in Chicago had an aging effect on a man. Though forty-nine years old, his face was as wrinkled as someone twelve-years older. The job had cost him more than his youth. His left ring finger was still slightly pale behind the knuckle where it had been covered for ten years. Constant mandatory overtime shifts kept him away, and it got to the point where his ex was counting on it, as he found out one day after being let off early for once. It seemed like a gift until he got home and found her nude with another man. In *his* bed!

Both his professional and personal lives had become a living hell. The only good thing about it was that it led to a job search, which concluded with him transferring to the sleepy town of Oak Grove. Despite its name, there was hardly any nonsense he had to deal with. The local population was only two-hundred-and-seventy-three, and most were folks who just wanted to keep to themselves. Occasionally outsiders would come in and start trouble, but for the most part, he could patrol around town, do some administrative work in his office…and spend the other thirty-five hours of the week playing online chess. If he could get an internet signal, that is.

He exited out of his current game and bitterly fixed his shirt with one hand while talking on the phone.

"Did he say where exactly?... Spruce Trail? Where exactly on the Spruce Trail? It zigzags all along the—Oh! About a half mile from the lake?... Okay, I know where to find him. No, don't call the State yet. Let me make sure this isn't some hoax. I'll keep in touch over the radio…Mmhmm...Thanks. Bye."

He hung up, finished tucking his grey police shirt in, then stood up out of his chair. He walked into the briefing lobby and immediately saw Deputy Russell Linn stuffing his face with a hot dog.

The twenty-four-year-old faked embarrassment when he turned and saw the Chief looking his way. His attempt to cover the mustard stain on his collar had failed miserably.

At least it hadn't dribbled down the whole front of his shirt this time.

"Hey, Chief," Russ said. "Heading in for the weekend?"

"Throw that thing away and come with me," Walter said. Russ was taken aback by the seriousness in his voice. Walter was typically a laid back chief, especially on Fridays. It was symptomatic of his satisfaction of leaving his Chicago life behind him in favor of the lush, quiet landscape of Oak Grove, Maine.

For a moment, Russ thought he was in trouble. But Walter wasn't walking back to his office—he was heading out for the back door, for the parking lot. Russ tossed the uneaten half of his hotdog in the trash and hurried after him, wiping his face with his wrist.

Walter walked at a brisk pace for his pickup truck.

"What's going on?"

"Possible homicide near the lake," Walter said. Russ' eyes bulged. He stopped briefly, only to be spurred by the 'what-the-hell-are-you-waiting-for' look by Walter. "Where's Shane and Christine?"

Russ shrugged. "Probably patrolling."

Walter snickered. "Yeah I'm sure." He buckled himself in and dug for his speaker mic. *Those two think I'm not aware.* He forced the thought from his mind. Now was not the time to address it.

CHAPTER 4

Christine laughed as she felt Shane Alter's lips press against her neck. They had been in the back of his Police Interceptor for the past ten minutes, which was strategically hidden in the woods on the southeast end of town. The only civilization on this end of Oak Grave was the Bixby Gas Station. Other than that, nobody wandered over this way after six in the afternoon.

"You're so bad," she said, feeling Shane's hand move over to her hip. He broke away from her, but only to let her see his mischievous smile.

"Rocking on the clock," he quipped. He moved in for another kiss. Christine Huron felt his hand going for her hair tie. Her natural desires were overwritten by a sense of urgency. She slapped his hand away.

"Easy there, mister. I know where your head's at."

"It's always there," Shane replied. Christine chuckled, accepted another kiss, then broke away. Shane reluctantly took the hint. "Alright, alright." He sat up straight and stared over the driver's seat through the windshield. As he waited for the stiffness to settle, he watched the wind brushing the red and brown colored leaves.

Christine smoothed her uniform and glanced back. Despite knowing the townsfolk pretty well, the slight fear that they may be caught still lingered in the back of her mind.

"The community's tax dollars at work," Shane joked, reading her mind. Christine chuckled.

"Be careful there, *Sergeant*," she said.

"I wish you'd call me that more," he said, nudging against her.

"ONLY on the job," she retorted.

"We *are* on the job!"

"You really are letting your new promotion go to your head," Christine said. She let him kiss her again. "You know..." she paused, interrupted by another kiss, "Shane, we're gonna have to go public at some point."

THAT was the way to kill the mood for Shane. He sighed, then felt a desire to stand up suddenly. Christine wondered if it was the wrong thing to say when he stepped out of the vehicle. She got out on her side then leaned over the trunk.

"Shane, even in this town, we can only keep our relationship quiet for so long. Eastman will find out eventually, if he hasn't already."

"I know, I know," Shane repeated. He rubbed his hand over his buzzcut, then reached into the driver's seat for his police ballcap. He felt silly for feeling this anxiety. It made him feel like a teenager who was overly obsessed with his first girlfriend. Rather than sixteen and naïve, Shane was thirty-one and apprehensive—BECAUSE he wasn't naïve. He knew how Walter would react to their relationship, especially with Shane obtaining the rank of Sergeant. "Not only does the department look down on employees hooking up, but now I'm technically a superior. If Walter finds out, you'll be moved to second shift."

"Probably," Christine said. Even though she believed in facing reality, it still depressed her to understand the depths of their decision. And unfortunately, their necking on the edge of town only proved Walter's reasoning for separating them. "And we'd never see each other, except on our days off...if they match up."

Shane turned around to look at her. He studied her figure, from her almond-brown ponytail down to the tip of the wilderness sleeve tattoo that protruded from the cuff of her right sleeve. She was always a country girl who enjoyed hiking, climbing, hunting, and fishing in the mountains. Shane too enjoyed many of these activities, particularly the fishing. Maybe it was her competitive personality that past girlfriends lacked that made him value this relationship more. Usually, at the three-month mark, he knew he was ready to move on to someone else. But Christine? He had been with her four months, and it was still as exciting as when they first hooked up. Distance and time apart was the ultimate killer of relationships, and making theirs known would likely ruin everything.

"We could always move," Christine said.

"Move?! *WE?!*" Shane exclaimed. As much as he valued the relationship, he wasn't ready for that kind of talk. Hell, he hadn't even gotten around to using the L-word, which Christine had been trying to get out of him for the last couple of weeks. Again, usually when that came up, it usually led to, "yeah, I'll see you later," which then led to a breakup. But somehow, Christine's pestering didn't have that effect.

"Yeah. I said it," she said.

"I just made Sergeant," Shane replied.

"In the town of Oak Grave! I think Detroit cops make more than we do," Christine said. He looked at her, then away. She sighed, reached into her pocket, then stuffed a cigarette between her teeth. "Want one?" She lit the tip, saw no response from him, then decided to offer it by hand.

Shane glanced down at it, then back up at her, then took one. He leaned over the trunk to let her light the tip for him.

"I like it here," he said. "I'm not really interested in going anywhere else."

"There's plenty of country towns that need deputies," she replied.

"Not as laid back as this," Shane said. Christine shook her head, resisting to call him out on his bullshit. *You think you're too accustomed to this job to pursue something more.* She understood Walter's reasoning. The guy had seen and done a lot and it showed in his face. He absolutely needed the rest. Christine, however, was still relatively early in her law-enforcement career and wanted something more, and though Shane wouldn't admit it, she suspected he felt the same way. He was turned down for jobs in Hancock County and Somerset County, and through good timing and luck, he managed to get this position. Though it was laid-back enough, Christine knew neither of them were living up to their full potential. She certainly didn't want to work in a big crime-infested city, and she loved the country. Oak Grave was just *too* quiet for her liking.

"Unit Two, come in."

Shane checked his watch, then answered his radio.

"Chief? Shouldn't you be in your polka dot pajamas right about now?" He looked at Christine and they shared a laugh.

"I need you and Christine to head over to the Spruce Trail in the forest grounds. We've received a report of a homicide. At the very least, it sounds like a missing person's report. I'm on my way with Russ right now."

Their laugh ended abruptly. Shane tossed his cigarette aside and quickly got into the driver's seat.

"Ten-four, Chief. I'm on my way." He started the engine as Christine got into the passenger seat.

"Unit Four copies," she radioed. Suddenly, she was starting to regret her feelings about Oak Grave being too quiet.

CHAPTER 5

It only took a few minutes for Shane and Christine to drive through town. The main road took them across the Cogburn's Bar, Brad Zink's grocery store, the Johnson Hotel, another local gas station, and the Local Eatery—whose name Christine initially thought was a joke when she first arrived. To the south, east, and west sides were all farmland and woods. Finally, there was Oak Grave Forest, whose twenty-three square miles of trees took up the bulk of the town's geography.

The main road intersected with William Drive, a dirt road that ran parallel with the southern edge of the forest. They followed the road for a quarter-mile until they saw the crooked sign which read *Spruce Trail*. The wooden plank was rotted and the letters of the word 'Trail' were barely visible.

Shane hit the windshield wipers to brush away a group of red maple leaves that rained on the Interceptor. He brought the vehicle to a near-stop then turned right onto the trail. A moment later, there was nothing but forest all around them.

The Spruce Trail was barely wide enough for a vehicle. Civilian vehicles were not permitted past the sign, and even the Chief was reluctant to drive here, as it was difficult to find a decent place to turn around other than the lake area. However, considering the distance the crime scene reportedly was from

William Drive, it would take too much time and remaining sunlight to go by foot.

"Would you hit the flashers for me?" Shane asked Christine. The red and blue strobes reached between the trees.

Christine was nibbling her fingertip. She was getting nervous and really could use a cigarette. Maybe when they got out to search, she could light one up. The vehicle bumped as it passed over a series of roots, then went down a small hill before curving to the left. These ups and downs and right and lefts were another reason vehicles were not typically allowed on the trail.

"How the hell do the Beasleys get around living this far into the forest?" she muttered.

"They're old school," Shane said, carefully steering the interceptor to the right. "They mainly ride horses whenever they go into town."

"Wish we had horses right now," Christine said. The path led them up another hill. The tires spun freely for a brief moment as they hit loose dirt, causing both officers to jump in their seats. The vehicle jolted as it found traction. After completing the short climb, they found themselves going straight forward for a good distance.

Christine glanced over at the mileage. They had gone a couple of miles into the forest so far. It would be another three miles before they made it to the lake. She gripped her seat and endured the rest of the trip, which continued in a series of tight bends clearly not designed with vehicles in mind.

"Maybe we should've taken Hosley Road. It connects with the dirt path that leads to the Beasley property. We could've cut through the woods from there, got around the lake and found the other end of the Spruce Trail," she said.

"You hear how long it took you to even explain that?" Shane replied. "It would've taken us too far to the west. This is the most direct route. Plus, I'm not sure if the Beasleys want a bunch of cop cars parking on their Ranch, while we search the trails."

Christine groaned. "It figures we don't have dirt bikes. Or ATVs." she replied.

"Gotta love the no-budget police department," Shane said. "Hell, why do you think our vehicles are ten years old?"

Walter Eastman's voice blasted through the radio.

"Unit One and Five are on scene."

"Unit Six to One, you want me and Three to assist?" It was Deputy Stevenson's voice. Shane was somewhat surprised that the round-bellied idiot even volunteered. He snuck a glance toward Christine. *Eh, who am I to talk? I'm the idiot who spent the last twenty minutes making out while on duty.*

"Remain on standby," Walter replied. *"Two? What's your status?"*

"Almost there, Chief," Shane said.

The trail straightened out after another two miles. They could see the Chief's flashers up ahead. As they closed within fifty yards, they could see Walter and Russ Linn speaking with two hunters.

Shane pulled up behind the pickup and parked. They stepped out and approached the group. Russ was the first to acknowledge them. He was the youngest member of the department, and it showed in his demeanor. He was jittery, unable to stand still while listening to the witnesses, whose backs were turned toward Shane and Christine while speaking with Walter.

"—I tried looking around, but there's no trace other than here," the taller one said. Walter took a couple of notes then glanced at the Sergeant.

"Alright, let's take a look."

The hunters turned to look, the taller one doing a double take after seeing Christine.

"Oh!" Christine said. "Robert."

"Hey," he said. He heard she had gotten a job in this county, but didn't realize it was in this tiny neck of the woods. He noticed Shane's questioning glances.

"You two know each other?"

"Uh, yeah," Christine replied. Shane recognized the tone, and Robert recognized the brief look of jealousy, which was duplicated and enhanced in his own facial expression. *Was she involved with this guy? Our engagement ended six months ago and she's already moved on?*

It took everything to keep these questions from spilling out into words. He sucked in a deep breath.

Not the time…

Robert stepped aside as the cops proceeded into the woods. "It's back there," he said, trying to shift his demeanor. Jake Cobb was biting his lip.

Great. Now I'm gonna have to listen to a dozen rants whenever we get back to the cabin. God only knows when that'll be. That led to a new series of thoughts. *Do we really want to go back to the cabin? Here, in the middle of nowhere? With a possible killer on the loose?*

They followed the officers into the trees, then waited as they arrived at the scene. Christine stopped and clutched Shane's hand. There was blood *everywhere*. She quickly let go.

Walter was kneeling by the rifle. He put on a rubber glove then picked the weapon up. It was completely crushed and bent, but with no sign of residue from trees. In fact, there was hardly any scraping at all on the metal. Had it been smashed against a tree, there'd be small groves all along the frame and muzzle. But it was clean. The Chief's puzzlement was plain on his face.

"It's almost—" he paused, realizing what he was about to say was going to sound silly, but it was the truth— "like someone grabbed it by the end and crunched it down by hand."

"There's tears on the Carhart," Shane pointed out.

"Yeah, but where's the body?" Russ said.

"Until we *find* a body, we must assume this gentleman might still be alive," the Chief said.

"On that note, you might find this detail important, Chief," Robert Windle said. He pointed at the bullet hole high up in the tree further south. Walter moved closer to inspect it, immediately realizing it was too high for the shooter to have been aiming at a deer, or even a man. And by the placement of the bullet, and the caliber, it was unlikely he was shooting a squirrel.

"It is," Walter replied.

Shane continued to inspect the jacket. The left arm was almost entirely ripped off. Interestingly, that was where the most blood had caked the inside. As though it was ripped away along with the arm that was in it.

Christine was gripping her Glock while she pressed further to the northwest. There was a wall of trees in her way. The ground had been carpeted by the leaves they had shed for the fall. She saw shades of orange, red, and brown all over the place.

And one speck of grey. Whatever it was, it wasn't tree or plant based. In fact, it was covered in fur. She moved closer, her eyes glancing into the surrounding forest. A breeze swept past her, causing the branches to sway.

Each movement felt like it made her heart stop. It was as though every figure in these woods wanted to come alive and take her away. It was moments like these that made her aware of her relative inexperience in the police force. She had been in the woods all her life, but never with a potential killer lurking nearby. She was used to being the hunter, not the other way around.

Like the Chief said, let's not jump to assumptions yet. Perhaps there wasn't a killer. Maybe the missing hunter injured himself, or got attacked by a moose or mountain lion. If so, he might've wandered to the Beasley Ranch. Except, that didn't explain the bent rifle. However, it would explain the bullet mark. Mountain lion jumped him from behind, took him by surprise, causing his rifle to jerk upward and discharge a shot…

Yeah, yeah, that actually made sense…

Her mental analysis came to an abrupt halt when she stood over the thing in the ground. Stripped fur on the tail was reminiscent of a racoon, as were the muscular tone and fur on its back legs. There was nothing beyond that other than some blood coated ribs and spinal column. The skeleton was fully intact, save for a couple of broken ribs, and the head, complete with its skin and eyes crushed like grapes, was flattened, as though caught in a vice.

"Guys?"

Shane was the first to hurry by her side. Right behind him was Robert, who sprinted with intense urgency after detecting the distress in her voice. Russ waited by the Carhart, while the Chief went to inspect the new finding.

It was definitely a racoon. All the meat had been stripped away. It looked as though the thing had been eaten like a drumstick.

Walter swallowed. There was no doubt in his mind that there was a connection between this and the missing person. What that connection was, he wasn't sure, and part of him didn't want to know.

"I should probably let you know we found a mutilated deer further back," Robert said. The Chief and officers looked at him.

"Like this?" Shane asked.

"Maybe worse," Robert replied.

"Mr. Windle, I want you and your friend to wait here," Walter instructed. "Officers, expand your search. We don't have much daylight remaining."

The group branched out. Robert begrudgingly waited at the crime scene, his eyes fixated on Christine walking beside Shane. It was almost as though she was seeking protection from the bastard. *The bastard...*Robert realized he didn't even know Shane and had already passed his verdict. Another swell of anger passed when he saw her light up a cigarette. *I had just about gotten her to quit.* Then Shane lit one up as well. *Now I know why she fell off the wagon.*

Jake Cobbs stepped beside him.

"Stop it, man."

"Stop what?"

"*It.* Just stop."

Robert took a breath. Either his thoughts were evident in his body language and facial expression, or Jake had telepathy. He turned on his heel and gazed into the woods around them. His jealousy was accompanied with fear. Something had happened to Lou, and it wasn't good. Whatever happened, it did not resemble the actions of some animal. The only conclusion he could think of was some crazy psychopath. Now, his fiancé...EX-fiancé—he had a hard time with the 'ex' part-was trekking into the woods where this possible psycho was lurking.

Those feelings worsened when she walked out of sight.

CHAPTER 6

They walked for a quarter-mile, checking in every few minutes with the Chief and Russ, who expanded their search to the southwest. Already, the radio frequency was crackling up. His last radio check, Shane had to speak twice before being heard.

Barren branches hung from the trees like demonic claws. Christine lit up another cigarette. The oral fixation was the only thing managing her stress right now. Shane was slightly better adjusted. He had been on one manhunt in the past, assisting the County Sheriff's Department in searching for a hit-and-run suspect. Then again, that person wasn't armed, and was mainly hiding out of fear. *This* was more than a little different. The smell of tobacco was stirring his craving for another cigarette.

The wind kicked up, knocking leaves from their branches, which rained down over the two officers. Christine was watching the branches. She was still thinking of mountain lions.

"We should've brought the shotgun from the Interceptor."

"Maybe," Shane replied, "but there's no use going back. Let's keep going."

"I don't see anything," she said. In a way, that was a relief. In another way, it wasn't. The longer it took to find something, the longer they'd be stuck out here. Being stuck out here in the woods at night was not a desirable predicament. "You think Walter will alert the County?"

"If we don't find anything, then probably." He gave in to the urge and lit another cigarette. He twirled the butt of his smoked cigarette between his fingers, looking for a place to discard it. He hated littering, but with the situation at hand, he didn't want to be distracted with having garbage filling up his pockets. He made an exception and tossed the thing into the woods. The yellow-stained filter bounced against the trunk of a tree and settled in the middle of a bunch of twigs sticking out of the ground like weeds.

He found himself staring at them. Normally, he wouldn't think anything of it. Perhaps it was the odd situation they were investigating. Perhaps he was looking too far into it, but these twigs weren't dead. They looked like the extensions from a branch that had broken off. Yet, there was no branch...though, judging by the frayed expansion of where one had broken off from the tree, there *had been* a branch here.

"What are you doing?" Christine asked.

"You see that?" he said, pointing. She went to inspect the twigs. They still held their leaves. The inside layers were shades of green. Definitely not dead wood. The broken ends were frayed, as though recently pulled off the limb they belonged to. Yet, the branch was non-existent. And by the way it had come off the tree, it wasn't a clean break. In fact, the way the bark was hanging from the bottom side, it was definitely *pulled* off.

"Should we radio it in?" she asked.

Shane shook his head. What would they say? 'Hey, Chief, we've got a missing tree branch out here.'

"Any progress?"

Speak of the devil...

"Negative. Well... uh," Shane briefly considered mentioning the discovery, "never mind."

"Five and I are heading back to the cars. There's nothing out here, and if we're gonna find anything, we're gonna need more people. You might as well head back too."

"Shane?" Christine said. "What if the missing person was injured and trying to make his way to the ranch?"

"He'd probably have gone this way," Shane replied.

"Well, it can be hard to know exactly where you're going when you're in these woods and not on the trail. What if he went for the lake? It's dead ahead to the north. There, it'd be easier to find the Phoenix Trail, which goes right by the Beasley Ranch. It's slightly longer, but a simpler route with less twists and turns. And when you're injured and disoriented, you probably would want the simplest method of finding help."

Shane thought about it for a moment.

"Chief?"

"Go ahead."

"We're already close to the lake. We're gonna see if the missing person might've gone back that way."

"Not a bad idea. Keep in radio contact. The wind's picking up."

"Ten-four." Shane glanced at Christine. She was already halfway down her cigarette. "You ready?"

She took another draw, nodded, then smiled nervously.

"I'm starting to feel stupid for that lecture I was giving you earlier," she said. "You know? About moving on to bigger and better things." She looked at the tree where the branch had been. "This doesn't look like the work of a person, but then again, I don't know how else to explain it."

Shane rubbed her shoulder. "It's probably nothing."

Christine nodded, though the gesture didn't put her at ease. She wanted it to be nothing, but the evidence didn't line up with that conclusion. A missing person, a rifle bent like a horseshoe, a racoon stripped to the bone, a deer in similar condition. Now, a branch ripped from its tree. She brushed her feet over the fallen leaves along the ground. There were traces of bark everywhere in the top layer. Considering the rate in which the leaves were coming off the tree, this happened recently.

She was tempted to continue with her weapon drawn, but she didn't trust herself with the nervous tension she was now experiencing. The darker shades of light shining through the grey sky weren't helping. She would probably shoot the first thing she saw move at this point.

"I could use a glass of wine by a fireplace," she said.

"I can arrange that," Shane said. He brushed a finger over her smooth chin. Finally, a genuine smile. It helped to have something to look forward to after all this craziness was over with.

She snapped into focus.

"This way's north," she said, pointing ahead. Shane followed her, then stopped momentarily after noticing several twigs scattered along the base of the next tree over. The lowest hanging branch on this one had also been torn free. Christine didn't take notice and was moving further away. Despite the temptation to inspect it, logic determined that he would find nothing new other than the other torn branch.

He quickened his pace to catch up with Christine.

CHAPTER 7

Robert Windle was tempted to pace back and forth. He was looking into the forest nonstop, in search of any human figures stepping out. The Chief had already updated him on what was happening, which only made his nervous energy worse. There were so many thoughts and emotions going through his head. Fear for Christine; jealousy and hate for that officer she was with; questions on whether she was actually hooking up with him—he could tell they were together, but there was a burning need for confirmation; a sickening feeling that something had happened to his buddy Lou, and the anxiety that a potential psychopath was lurking in this forest.

There was menace behind every falling leaf, every swaying branch. The wind taunted them. Worse, the Chief was trying to radio his dispatcher, only to receive static. Their radios were practically as old as every building in town.

"Dispatch, you get that? Over." More static. "Damn it." Walter was regretting not following a temptation months earlier to simply spend his own money on better quality radios. The minute he got home, he'd be getting online to look some up. He gave up, then turned to look at the two hunters.

"Gentlemen, I appreciate your help. You're free to go home if you wish."

Both Jake and Robert shook their heads.

"Uh, no offense, Chief, but our ATV is a mile or so up that way," Jake pointed southeast, "and frankly, I'm not comfortable with walking through these woods with, uh..."

"A killer wandering about," Robert finished his sentence.

"We can help you get to your cabin," Walter said.

"I appreciate that, Chief, but Jake's point still stands. Being in a cabin all night, with barely any radio or phone contact, while someone might be lurking out here..."

Walter sighed. He hated the idea of babysitting civilians on a crime scene, but time was at stake, and it would take a while just to get the cars turned around. Then there was the slow trip to take them back to town, then to come back. It was faster than on foot, but not by much.

"Alright, fine. Just wait here." Walter moved back toward the trail for another try on the radio. "Dispatch?" Nothing. "Russ, you give it a try."

Russ Linn tried radioing, but only got static.

"We need a more open area," he said.

"Maybe we'll try the Beasley Ranch after Robert and Christine check in," Walter said. He groaned. "I hope those two aren't fucking around up there."

Jake watched as Robert tensed. It was practically confirmation to what he already suspected.

Get over her, please...

****

A month or so back, the shore of McCluskey Lake would have been teeming with dragonflies, frogs, and various other critters. Now, those that did not flee to warmer parts of the globe during the winter were in the process of digging new burrows where they would reside until spring. The cattails turned a shade of grey, and the tree line on the opposite side of the lake was almost barren, except for the pines.

Shane and Christine arrived in the clearing at the end of the trail. There was roughly a hundred feet of open space, which led to a few wood benches and a dock that extended twenty feet into the lake.

The two officers were anticipating a calming sight, as both were outdoors people, and loved being near lakes and ponds. But rather than the gentle swells rippling to shore, their eyes were fixed on the unattended fishing rod and tacklebox on the dock.

The rod was propped on a steel post and was bending severely. There was a fish snagged on the line trying to escape. Had it not been for the post, the rod would have been yanked clear into the water.

There was nobody around.

"Hello?" Shane called out. His hope was that perhaps the owner was in the woods taking a leak.

Christine approached the dock. She stopped. Some of the planks were busted, as though a massive sledgehammer had been brought down on them. That, or something as heavy as a grizzly stepped onto the dock.

Now, their pistols were drawn.

Shane approached the dock, half-anticipating to see a body on the shore or floating in the water. Christine looked into the water, saw no evidence, then looked down the lake in each direction. The lake had a curvy shape to it, arching northwest for a quarter mile past the Beasley property.

Shane was on the dock. The rod was near the end, the fish still tugging at the line. There was supposed to be a bench at the end of the dock. All that remained were the torn wooden stumps connecting to the dock itself. Several planks were crushed leading up to it; about every third or fourth one. He arrived at the end and peered into the water. The lake was shallow, offering a clear view of the bottom. Propped in the weeds was a blue bait container, a white bucket for carrying catch, pieces of the wooden bench, along with scattered items spilled from the tacklebox.

"Shane?"

He didn't quite register Christine's voice as he studied the discarded items. Clearly, not thrown in on purpose. They had fallen in during a struggle. He looked back and around, finding no sign of the owner.

"Shane?"

He knelt down to inspect the posts for the bench. The beams were snapped off like toothpicks. "The fuck?"

"Shane?!"

He looked this time. "Yes?"

She was pointing at something in the cattails, roughly thirty feet left of the dock. Some of the cattails were bent over, weighed down by some sort of mass.

"There's something in there…"

Shane gave one last glance at the items in the water, then hurried back to shore. Christine was slowly approaching the cattails. He could see the bulk of something in the middle, somewhat submerged in the water. The surrounding cattails obscured any direct view of what it was.

He gently reached toward Christine and lowered her gun toward the ground, then approached the vegetation. There was something protruding from the mass—jagged bony extensions. Antlers? Another dead deer?

Shane holstered his Glock then leaned over to grab them. He could see the head of the deer propped between the cattails. Probably a hundred pounds of meat. He pulled, anticipating such weight, and was surprised when it was only fifteen pounds. He fell backward, the severed head of the deer scraping along the grass.

"Oh, Jesus," Christine exclaimed. Shane let go of the thing and scurried back. As he fumbled for his radio, Christine was glancing all around them. "Shane, this isn't normal."

"I know," he said.

"No, I mean, this REALLY isn't normal," she said. "There's nothing in these woods that would do that. There's no grizzlies or brown bears. Black bears couldn't do this. There's nothing here that could rip the head off a deer like it's a bottle cap."

"Hold it together," he said. He fumbled for his radio. "Chief?"

"Go ahead."

"Can you head over to the lake? We've, uh… we found… just come over here. It'll be simpler."

"On my way."

Christine looked up at Shane and shook her head with worry. "What's going on here?"

He, in turn, shook his head.

"I don't know. I really…just don't know."

CHAPTER 8

"Unit One to Dispatch?" Walter Eastman gazed at the broken bench and fishing contents in the water as he spoke in the radio.

"Go ahead, Chief."

Finally! He was able to get through.

"Can you get in touch with the State and ask if they can send some troopers out here. Let them know we have at least two missing persons. And check for any alerts sent from hospitals. Specifically, mental hospitals."

"Y-yes, Chief. Will do."

He could hear the confusion in her voice.

"Something's not adding up out here. I don't want to jump to conclusions, but from my experience, it's pointing to a homicidal maniac. Yes, tell that to the State. I want a senior officer out here."

"Ten-four."

"Chief, you want us to come out there?" It was Deputy Stevenson again.

"Yes, please. Be careful on the trail," Walter replied.

"On our way."

The Chief clipped his speaker mic back to his shirt collar and stared at the scene. Russ stood near the department's pickup, while the hunters were inspecting the deer stump.

"I've hunted and gutted deer all my life, Chief. I can tell you; this was not done with any blade," Robert Windle said.

"Spinal column's all twisted," Jake Cobb said. "I can't tell you who or what did that."

"Chief?" Christine raised her hand. "May I recommend one of us take the witnesses back into town? We don't know exactly who we're dealing with out here, and…no offense guys, but looking after civilians out here will only make our job a little more difficult."

Robert scoffed.

"Can't stand being around me, huh?"

"That's not it, Robert…" Christine said.

"Yeah, then what is it?"

"It's exactly what I said."

Shane glanced back and forth between the two. The tension between them was wire-tight the instant they met. It wasn't long before Shane started doing the math.

She had mentioned being engaged previously. Is this guy…?

"Well, I'm not going back to the cabin," Jake said. "I'll never sleep."

"Same here," Robert added. His brief glance toward Christine didn't go unnoticed. She looked away. The guy was an egotistical prick, but he had protective instincts that were second to none. And clearly, he had not gotten over their failed relationship.

He slung his rifle over his shoulder. "No offense, but can any of you guys even shoot worth a damn?"

Shane shot him a glare, which Christine also noticed. Whether it was for the remark, or a male dominance thing over protecting his mate, she wasn't sure. Probably both.

"Just so happens I can. You?"

"I'll neuter a fruit fly with this thing," Robert retorted.

"Knock it off," Walter said with authority. The shoreside went silent. Robert and Shane stared each other down for another moment, then each turned away. Walter slowly exhaled. He, too, could tell there was a history between Christine and Robert that was rearing its ugly head. The fact that it was doing so even during a serious investigation such as what they were currently

THE BLOOD OF BIGFOOT

conducting spelled trouble. Christine was right; they didn't have the time to be looking after tourists while conducting this investigation.

He glanced over at Russ. "Linn, when Stevenson and Flowers get here, take these guys back to the station."

Jake was fine with that, while Robert wore a scowl on his face.

"There's other trails here? Can't we just ride back down one of those?" Jake asked.

"They're even narrower than this one," Walter explained. "The Spruce Trail here is the only one our vehicles can fit through. Everything else, unless you're on a four-wheeler or bike, you're stuck on foot."

Jake grimaced. *Damn, I wish we didn't leave the ATV back at the campsite.*

"Just bear with us a while. We'll get you out of here shortly," Walter said.

"Not soon enough," Christine muttered under her breath. She turned and walked away, pretending to be looking for additional clues. She heard footsteps behind her. Shane. He was glancing back at the hunters, then gave her a questioning look.

"Is that him?" he whispered.

She sighed. "Before I took this job, we used to come out here to hunt."

"Oh..." His voice was slightly inquisitive, like he didn't believe that was all it was.

"It's *over*," she said. "He hadn't come up here in years. He had found places he seemingly liked more. I didn't think he'd come back when I took this job. And even if I had, he'd be in the woods. We're usually in the town and farming areas. If this didn't happen, we wouldn't have even known the other was here."

"Looks like he's not quite over it," Shane said.

"It's been a tough year for him. He's not a bad guy. Just... pushy."

Shane detected emphasis in that last word, and quickly read between the lines. It was not just an exposition of what drove her and Robert apart, but a reality check of how Shane was now acting.

A flock of cardinals took off into the sky from deep within the forest, drawing the attention of the group. They watched in silence as the birds took off high into the sky and retreated north.

"Not quite the way they want to go for winter," Russ said.

"No… it isn't," Walter said. He hated looking too deep into minor occurrences. Birds flocking wasn't normally something that would hold his attention. But he couldn't help but notice the speed and direction. It was a retreat. Something had spooked them out of hiding. He didn't hear any gunshots from other hunters possibly in the area.

Probably nothing.

He inhaled deeply and watched the mouth of the trail, eager to see Officer Stevenson's Interceptor emerge from around the bend.

****

Officer Beau Stevenson regretted offering his assistance by the third hill. Twice now, he nearly hit a tree. Doing this gave him a new respect for the Chief, whom he had heard make remarks about getting four-wheelers or motorcycles for the department, specifically for navigating these trails properly. Of course, there wasn't much in the way of tax dollars from the tiny population Town Hall drained it from, thus there wasn't much funding to maintain the equipment they had, let alone update it.

In the passenger seat was Edward Flowers, a dark-skinned man in his upper thirties. His physical inactivity was displayed in the potbelly he developed in his two years of working in the department after moving from Wisconsin. He was no stranger to wooded areas, nor was he unfamiliar with searching for missing persons in such locations.

In his past job, he was often posted in the state parks, which had deep trails such as this. At least a few times a year, somebody would get lost. And in his fifteen years there, they had at least two cases of possible deceased persons in the woods. The first was a suicide, which led to a week-long search before the body was discovered. The second was more haunting, being a first-degree murder with a knife. Those thoughts were flooding back to him as he watched the endless series of trees passing by. Every time they passed by a decent spacing between the trees, his eyes planted the image of someone fleeing through the woods, wearing a shirt caked in blood. It was the only glimpse he caught of the guy, who was rounded up a couple of days later by the State Police.

Beau Stevenson was a few years younger. Unlike Ed, he had been here all of his life, and his girth made his partner look like a triathlete. Ten years ago, when he first hired on, he was twenty-four years old and lean. Then, he fell into a routine of sitting all day, eating too many chili dogs and pizzas, and watching sports rather than playing them. His separation from his wife only exacerbated the issue, especially when he discovered Facebook photos of her and her new boytoy on some beach. Judging by that smile on her face, and how her hand was on his ripped abdomen in every photo, Beau knew there was zero chance of winning her back. With his woman gone, and his eating habits having turned him unattractive to boot, there was only the love of food to keep him going.

Even now, his stomach was growling.

"How can you be hungry?" Ed asked. Beau shrugged, his neck rippling under his chin as he scratched it.

"Why wouldn't I be?" he replied. "It was almost dinner time when the call came in."

"Didn't you *listen* to the call?" Ed asked.

"I did. Hence, I asked the Chief if he wanted our help. Just wish I packed a bag of chips or something for the road."

"This isn't a laughing matter."

"I didn't say it was," Beau replied. "You think my stomach's growling on my command?"

Ed chuckled. *Fair point.* Beau wasn't a bad guy by any stretch, nor did he even have a bad personality. And how could he be considered lazy considering he worked in a town that almost literally gave him nothing to do? Occasionally they'd visit the cabin rentals on request of the owner when tenants refused to move out on time, and occasionally they'd help with roadside assistance in the winter. When tourists arrived, they were usually the ones who helped with giving directions. Other than that, their daily activity was comprised of driving around while listening to baseball and football scores. It was a police station with very little police work. They often bragged that their jail was the cleanest in the state, deliberately leaving out the fact that it was vacant most of the time.

"Well, it's possible," he joked. His smile vanished when they passed another bend. The spacing was narrow, putting the passenger side mirror within inches of the trees. They could hear branches scraping over their heads. Being closer to the tree line, he couldn't help but peer into the woods. Once again, his mind played tricks on him.

"Couldn't this have happened at noon?" he muttered.

"No shit," Beau said, glancing up at the sky. By his estimation, there was maybe another hour of daylight left at best. It was NOT going to be fun maneuvering this Interceptor back through the trail at night. "With that said, I don't know how we're going to find this guy in these miles of woods at night. And God only knows how long it'll take the State to get up here. It's been so long since they've even heard from us, they've probably forgotten we exist."

He completed the turn around the bend, after which the trail straightened out.

"There," Ed pointed. Up ahead was Shane Alter's Interceptor. It was pulled over to the side, and even so, there was barely enough room to get around it. The spacing was so tight that Beau wasn't actually sure if his vehicle would fit around it. He rolled his window down and folded his mirror back to keep it from grazing the corner of Shane's. Even so, it still made a little contact, leaving a small scratch along the plastic. "Fabulous."

"Not like anyone will really notice," Ed said. They looked to the left at the length of yellow caution tape blocking off the section of woods. Ed sighed. "Guy's probably close by and they just missed him."

"He could be anywhere," Beau replied.

"Yeah. That's what makes me nervous. And with this breeze, with night falling, anything that moves could be either the missing persons or the suspect." A wind tore through the woods, blowing a wall of leaves against the windshield. "Case and point."

"Gosh, they're coming down early. Must be the cold," Beau said.

"Probably drives the trees crazy just like—LOOKOUT!"

It burst from the trees, its brown muscular body freezing when it saw the oncoming vehicle.

Beau reacted, hitting the brakes while instinctually turning the wheel to the left. The Interceptor collided with a tree, caving the grill several inches into the engine. Beau and Ed didn't even notice the smoke billowing from the hood, as both had turned back to look at the panicking horse stomping its hooves along the trail. It bucked and turned, looking back the way it came.

Beau opened his door to step out. "What the hell?" He fell back in as another horse came racing out of the woods. Like the first, it was bucking and neighing. Beau hurried out and raised his hands out, slowly approaching the creatures.

"Whoa! Whoa! Whoa!"

The horses gradually calmed. One still had its harness and reins on. It slowly approached the officer, who gently took it by the reins. Whatever was going on, it was clear that the horse was happy to be near a human.

Ed stepped out of the vehicle and inspected the engine.

"Damn it."

"Think Walter will notice *that*?" Beau muttered.

"He will when we tow it out," Ed said. He looked at how the vehicle was sticking out into the trail. "Crap! He's gonna have our asses. It's blocking the way. Now it'll REALLY take the State a hundred years to get out here. And all because of these dipshits. What are they doing out here anyway?"

"I recognize this one. They're from the Beasley Ranch," Beau said. Only when he said it did it register in his mind as strange. "What *are* you doing out here?" He glanced back into the woods. "And what were you running from?"

CHAPTER 9

"Well, you really did a number on this one," Walter said to Beau. The horses were still whinnying as the officer clung to the one with the reins. The other trotted back and forth, looking as though it would take off any moment.

"Whoa," Shane Alter said. His attempt to calm it down had limited effect. Even the one with the reins looked as though it would take off any moment.

"You see how they're acting?" Beau said. "They came shooting out in front of us as though the devil was after them."

"We're lucky we didn't hit one of *them*," Ed added. Walter sighed, then looked at the vehicle.

"Can we back it up and line it with the trees?"

"Already tried," Ed said. "Engine's dead. We could try pushing it, I suppose. Hope you're looking forward to throwing your back out when we try to line it up." Walter didn't laugh at the joke. Nor did any of the others.

Jake stood by the bed of the Chief's pickup truck, where he and Robert sat during the ride over. He was gnawing on his lip, his foot constantly brushing the ground. His anxiety was generating a lot of nervous energy, and the need to urinate wasn't helping matters.

"So… what are the odds we'll get a ride back?"

"Just…" Walter held a hand out, as though signaling for them to wait. *Wait* for his temper to mellow. He took a breath. "We can't yet. This is the only pathway wide enough for the vehicles, and we're gonna have to move it."

"What about the horses?" Christine asked.

"These belong to the Beasley Ranch," Shane added. "They NEVER let their horses go loose."

"Perhaps these guys were eager to get away from their owners?" Robert suggested.

"Not a chance," Beau said. "The Beasleys are good folks. They take good care of their animals. Not one case of abuse, if that's what you're implying."

"Yeah? Which way is their ranch from here?" Robert said. Beau pointed to the west. "And which way did them horses come running from?" Beau exhaled, then pointed again in the same direction.

"Son of a gun," Walter muttered. He got on his radio. "Dispatch?" He repeated the call, backing up the trail until he found a spot where his signal could break through. "Dispatch?"

"Here, Chief."

"Can you make a call to the Beasley Ranch? Make sure everything's alright. Let 'em know we have a couple of their horses, which were running loose over the Spruce Trail."

"Will do, Chief."

"It's not far from here. We might want to go check it out," Shane suggested.

"We might. Let's just wait a sec," Walter replied.

"I just don't see their horses getting loose like this," Shane continued. "Chief, I've seen them walking free rein with these guys. These are well-trained horses. They wouldn't just bolt from the pasture."

"Yes-yes, I get it, Shane," Walter said. "Like I said, give Dispatch a moment. And meanwhile, give me a second to figure out a game plan."

"How many horses do they have?" Jake asked.

"Six, I think," Beau answered. "Horses, cows, goats, chickens, they have a whole farm over there."

"Six, huh? Where are the others?" Robert said.

"I imagine back at the farm," Shane replied.

"Where these guys should be..." Walter muttered. He was sounding worried now, which by itself, worried his subordinates.

"Chief?"

"Yeah."

"I called twice, but they're not picking up."

"Fuck!" Walter said under his breath. He glanced at the crime scene, the end of the trail, and the horses. Normally, he would want to keep an officer at each sectioned off area, but something about splitting up didn't feel right. "Alright. Dispatch, call Harold. Tell him he's starting his shift early. I want him on Angel Drive to spot for the State Troopers if they ever show up. Tell him to bring them to the Beasley Ranch when they do."

"Will do, Chief."

Walter clipped his speaker mic and turned toward Beau. "You think you can tie the reins to a tree or something to keep him from wandering off?"

Beau nodded and led the horse to a tree a few yards up the trail. He found a firm branch, then started looping the reins around it.

The horse grunted, then yanked its head back.

"Whoa," he said, calmly. He proceeded to tie the knot. The horse whinnied again, then yanked its head back harder, undoing the progress he had made. "Whoa!" he said with more grit. He pulled back on the reins, which only served to agitate the horse more. It reared up on its hind legs, causing the pudgy officer to let go of the reins and stagger backwards. The other horse was now braying, running back and forth through the crowd.

Together, the horses disappeared eastward through the woods.

"Jesus!" Christine said.

"Looks like he didn't want you tying him up, Officer," Robert said.

"Like I said..." Beau brushed some residue off his uniform, "I know them horses. This isn't common. Y'all saw it. They're scared out of their minds."

Walter raised a hand to get the group's attention. "Alright, we're gonna go check out the ranch. I'll get the truck turned around, then pile into the bed and we'll head over to the lake. From there, we'll take the Phoenix Trail southwest, which'll take us near the Beasley Ranch."

"You seriously don't expect us to stay out here, do you?" Robert said. Walter hesitated before answering.

"You can come along, but you WILL take instructions from me or any of my officers. You can hang on to your weapons, but don't go out there acting like commandos. I don't need you shooting into the woods and getting yourselves or one of my officers killed. I appreciate your willingness to help, but you must follow the chain of command, which you're at the bottom of. Understood?"

"So, does this mean we're deputized?" Jake asked.

"Understood?" Walter said again.

"Yes...sir," Robert replied.

Jake stammered, then stood straight. "Yes, Chief."

"Good. Let's check out the Ranch."

CHAPTER 10

The Beasley Ranch was comprised of eight acres of land, surrounded by forest and rolling hills. To the south was the residence, a nice two-story building where the couple had raised three kids, who'd all grown and moved away by now. Behind it were the goat pen and chicken coop, and a hundred feet past that was the barn.

The barn was comprised of two main sections, one for housing the horses, the other for the cows. Behind the barn was four acres of fenced off pasture for the animals, again divided in half to separate them. At the end of the fence was a thin area of forest separating the ranch from the lake. On the east side, another thin patch of forest separated the ranch from the Phoenix Trail, where six police officers and two hunters were trekking southwest on foot.

Before they cut through the patch of trees, the group picked up on an odd mixture of smells. It was a mix of burnt barbeque, manure, and something that Beau Stevenson could only describe as rot. Jake and Robert had another word. They had hunted most of their lives, and knew the distinct smell of animal innards freshly exposed.

Walter Eastman was at the front of the group, his hand resting on his sidearm as he cautiously passed through the woods.

The sinking sun created long black shadows protruding from the base of each tree.

He emerged on the other side, like stepping through a theatre curtain onto a vast stage. They had emerged on the property, roughly halfway alongside the east pasture fence. Except, the section of fence directly in front of them was not standing. Ten feet of hotwire had been ripped from its post and crushed into the ground. The Chief did not look at the fence long enough to identify its dented, jagged form, as he was focused on what lay in the dirt beyond it.

Thus, he identified the origin of the deathly smell.

The horse was on its right side, its ribs and intestines sprawled out on the grass for several feet beyond its hooves. Its mouth was agape, the lips peeled back, revealing white teeth. The creature had died with a screaming neigh.

Several meters to the south was another. And another. And to the north, another. Four dead horses, and even more dead cows on the west pasture near a busted piece of drilling machinery. By the looks of it, the Beasleys were creating a new well for the animals. The well-digger had been impaled into the neck of one of the cows like a javelin, pinning it to the ground a few meters from the gaping hole.

Walter looked to his right. Near the northeast corner, a horse had its legs entangled in the fence. By the looks of it, it had tried to leap over the hotwire, but couldn't clear the height. Stuck in the mesh, it was trapped, and now dead as its flesh was peeled off—of which there wasn't much remaining.

The pasture was practically red with dried rivers of blood.

A hundred exclamations wrestled in Walter's mind to be vocalized, but none made it out. The last time the Chief found himself utterly speechless and in shock was on his third year on the job when a body was discovered in a trashcan. It had been there for months before someone finally reported the smell. The rotting thing under the lid could barely be described as human. And even with the sight and smell, the senior detectives were actually kidding with each other and even eating lunch while investigating the scene.

But even those detectives, if they were here, would probably not be so nonchalant. Not in the face of this massacre.

He unholstered his Glock, as did Shane and Christine. The other three officers kept their hands, which were trembling with anxiety, resting on their holsters. Up ahead directly to the west was the fence that separated the cow pasture. Much of it had been uprooted, the posts drawn out from the ground like weeds.

"Mountain lions, perhaps?" Robert broke the silence. He didn't believe it, but his mind would not rest on the 'what did this?' factor.

"I—" Shane shook his head. "No. They couldn't have."

"Stevenson, hold here. Let's make something of a perimeter," Walter said. He looked to the sky, which was gradually turning a darker shade of grey. Their natural light was running out fast. "Everyone else, head for the barn. Beau, if you see or hear anything, speak up."

"Don't have to tell me twice," Beau replied. His eyes were locked on the disemboweled horse while the cops and hunters moved south along the fence.

The posts were all leaning to the right, likely due to the force of the section being ripped away. Shane Alter took a moment to inspect the broken edges.

"It's literally been broken off. Not cut."

"Come on, Sergeant," Walter said.

They continued south and turned the corner, where the post had also been nearly ripped from the ground. The south side of the fence connected with the back of the barn, which allowed the Beasleys to let the animals directly into the pasture. The east side of the building appeared to be okay. The front side, however, was a different story. The doors were in pieces, the wooden fragments shaped like stakes in a vampire film. They were scattered across the dirt and the concrete floor of the barn.

Walter peered inside, Glock pointed. There was nothing there other than an empty aisle and equally empty horse stalls. There was dirt on the ground. Nothing unusual, as horses tracked dirt all the time when coming in for the night. But there was something distinctive about the clumps of dirt in this aisle. It was spaced apart...like footsteps. There wasn't quite a distinct shape, but the placement looked like a stride a man would take…a very large man.

That realization drew Walter's eyes to the dirt in front of the doors. He was hoping to see boot prints, some sort of indication of a psychotic maniac, which the evidence was pointing to at the moment. There were indeed prints, but they were not anything from footwear.

"You seeing this?" he muttered to the others. Robert moved through the crowd and kneeled at one of the more distinctive prints that wasn't brushed over by the struggle of wrecking the door.

Jake knelt down next to him, his face wrinkled as he stared dumbfounded by the print.

"It is…human?"

"I—" Robert shook his head, "…don't know." He held both index fingers to the print, one at the toe, the other at the heel. It was well over a foot long. "The toes are elongated, and by the looks of it, kinda jagged. Like bones. And whatever it was, it's at least as heavy as a male gorilla."

"A gorilla?" Ed chuckled. "You mean to tell me a big primate came through here? Did it take a canoe from Africa or something? Hitch a ride on a cruise ship?"

"I didn't say that's what it was, smartass," Robert growled.

"Maybe it's just a weird boot. Like one of those worn during ice climbing," Jake said.

Walter nodded. Though the idea didn't make sense on its own, it still lined up with the idea of a homicidal maniac, who often used unconventional methods of slaughter. Then again…

He looked down the aisle, through the open back doors, into the pasture.

Could one man really have done ALL of this? More questions whirled in his consciousness. *Who's to say it was only one person?*

The sound of rustling leaves and fluttering wings drew his attention to the woods on the west side. It was a small flock of doves taking to the sky. Scared? Or just flying off?

Don't overthink every detail. You'll drive yourself insane.

He took his mind off of it. Birds fly. What wasn't normal was the condition of this farm.

Shane was moving to the cow aisle, which had its own separate entrance, which was a smaller door. It was mostly intact, the center splintered as it lay on the concrete aisle, as though kicked off its hinges. He stepped inside. Like the horse aisle, most of the interior had been left untouched. Except one stall.

He remembered that the Beasleys had one cow that was sick, which they were temporarily keeping inside during its medical treatment. Its stall door had been ripped off its hinges and tossed to the back of the aisle. His brain registered the smell of intestines, which was much more permeating indoors. Christine followed him in, both hands gripping her Glock.

Shane lit his flashlight and proceeded.

The sick cow's suffering had ended, but not due to the illness that it was facing. Shane coughed, both from the smell and the sight of its bloody remains. Its limbs had been ripped from the body, leaving it a baggy, deflated corpse. There were bones lying about in the hay, some sticking out from the meat, almost resembling antennae wires on an old television.

He looked back at Christine, whose eyes met his.

"You find something?" Walter asked, peering through the entrance. Shane cocked his head into the stall.

Look for yourself.

He wandered to the back of the barn and glared at the pasture. His attempt to provide a brief respite from the carnage only resulted in him staring at more. Animals were dead everywhere, the fence torn apart in various sections. The only sense of normalcy was the water trough on the southwest perimeter. It had been filled that morning.

The investigation led to the goat and pig pens. The wire fence had been pulled apart, the posts uprooted with ease, considering they were smaller than those in the main pasture.

What struck Shane as odd was that, while there was a little blood, there were no bodies. Had the smaller animals managed to outrun their attacker?

The goats? Maybe. The pigs? That he doubted. Pigs were natural sprinters, but they would tire out easily. There should be at least ONE lying about. And it was hard to believe they'd escape something that four horses apparently couldn't get away from.

Only the chickens were left alive—some of them. There were feathers and crushed bodies along the coop, which had been knocked over and smashed. The stragglers scurried around, some clucking in a panic, some even flapping their wings. Born and raised here, they weren't going to leave the property, but it looked as though they wanted to.

Robert was sniffing.

"Notice something?" Jake asked. "Me too."

"What?" Russ Linn asked.

"There," Robert said. He pointed over at the back patio, near the back entrance. A four-burner grill stood, with black smoke billowing through the lid. The hunter approached and opened the lid, revealing four black burgers that almost looked like coal due to being so burnt. He switched off the propane tank. "I don't know the homeowner, but I think I can assume he's not the type that would let good meat go to waste. Or leave a grill running unattended for what I would guess would be an hour or so."

The Chief and his officers said nothing, and quickened their pace to get to the front entrance.

Walter took the lead as they turned the corner. They saw the driveway with a pickup truck on it, undamaged. The front of the house, however, way anything but normal. The flower garden had been partially stomped. In the dirt were more of those prints with the jagged toes, leading to the front door…or rather, where it used to be.

"This is the Oak Grove Police Department!" Walter announced. There was no answer.

"Chief?" Christine muttered.

"Keep calm," Walter said.

Now, Ed and Russ had their pistols drawn. Walter pointed at them and whispered, "Circle around the back." They did as instructed. Walter gestured at the two hunters to step back, to which they complied. The Chief glanced at Shane and Christine. "On me."

He turned and slowly entered the building.

"Police!" he repeated. "Anyone here? Hello? Mr. Beasley?!" As he passed through the empty door frame, he realized the top had been busted off, as though whoever came through was too big for it.

On the wall to his left was a bullet hole. Rifle caliber. He remembered that Mr. Beasley owned a Henry Rifle. Clearly, he fired a shot from somewhere in the living room area.

There it was, just beyond the corner leading into the staircase. On the floor between the door and bedroom was a smidgen of blood, some of it smeared by the strange footprints. Whose blood? Did Hobert Beasley land a shot? Or was it his blood?

There was no body around the corner. Nothing, other than cavities in the walls and ceiling.

"Up the steps," Walter instructed Shane and Christine. They rushed up the stairway into the bedroom, hopping over the steps that were broken.

They entered a hallway that led to three bedrooms. The two on the left were the guest bedrooms, formerly belonging to their now-grown children. They were empty, as was the master bedroom on the right. Like the main entrance, the top of the doorframe had been ripped away.

"Oh God," Christine muttered. The back window was busted, the shards on the floor beneath it crusted with blood and hair. No Hobert or Sandy Beasley. Shane knelt down by the shards of wood that previously was the door and located the knob. It was locked. One of them, likely Sandy, had tried to hide in here.

"Shane? Let's go," Christine said. He backed out of the room and followed her down the steps.

Walter had already checked the kitchen, bathroom, and utility areas. There was nobody here.

"Christ," Walter groaned. He hurried out the door and got on his radio. "Beau, you there?"

"Yeah, I hear ya."

"Get back up here. I don't want any of us separated at the moment," he said. "Dispatch?" There was a response, but it was muffled in static. "Goddamnit." He walked into the side yard. "Dispatch, come in please."

"I'm here, Chief."

"Call the State Police and tell them to get up here on the double," he said. "Direct them to the Beasley Ranch. We need forensics and…probably SWAT."

More static came in.

"Sorry, Dispatch, that last transmission did not come in." He moved again. "Try again."

More static… *"—not received, Chief."*

Jesus, Lord Almighty, why am I stuck with THESE stupid radios?!

"Dispatch—"

"Hey guys, look at this!" Robert called out.

Walter glanced around, realizing the hunter had wandered over to the west tree line, straight out from the edge of the cow pasture. Jake Cobbs was waving his hands to get their attention.

"Standby," Walter said on the radio, then hustled over with the others. The hunters were standing in the few feet of grassy space between the trees and the fence. Feathers and leaves swirled around them like bees after being kicked up by a small gust of wind, upsetting the chickens further.

Russ and Ed waited behind while Christine and Shane followed the Chief. Meanwhile, an out-of-shape Beau Stevenson hobbled across the yard, only to stop and gaze at the wreckage that was the pens.

It was about a hundred steps to where the hunters stood.

"Goddamnit, guys, you mind *not* wandering off? We have enough missing persons right now," Walter said. The hunters didn't reply. In fact, they looked sick. Robert pointed his rifle toward the base of a birch tree, which stood just a few meters below the tree line. Walter shone his flashlight and saw the red and black fabric of what appeared to be a jacket. A closer inspection made him realize it was the only arm of a jacket, with the arm still inside. The fingers were curled around an exposed root of the tree, the knuckles dislocated and pale. The inches of dirt around it had minor trenches caused by what had to be clawing at the ground.

Perhaps Walter had grown too used to the laid-back nature of his job. Perhaps he had lost his edge. All he knew was that he was feeling overwhelmed for the first time in decades. Every discovery was worse than the last, and on top of that, none of the answers made sense.

"Maybe we should get out of here," Jake said. "There's a truck. We could ride out in it. We can fit in the bed."

"No," Robert demanded, sparking a stern look from his cousin.

"Seriously, man? Look at this?"

"You yourself said we'd rather not head out on our own," Robert hissed.

"In the cabin, no, but I'm fine with heading to town." Jake said. He looked toward the house, or rather, the westside road that cut through the forest. "I say we take the truck and head into town."

Robert leaned over toward him. "We're not going anywhere."

"You can stay here and try to win back your ex. But I'm not hanging around." He looked to Shane. "You know where they keep the keys to the truck?"

"How the hell should I know?" Shane replied. His voice contained a combination of fear, exhaustion, and reluctance. There was simply too much to focus on. Too many questions and things to consider. Was it even okay to simply let Jake take the Beasleys' property? He felt like he should be stopping him. Normally, he would without a second thought, but this was an unprecedented situation. On one hand, it was pretty much certain they wouldn't be needing it, and part of him was anxious to get out of here as well. The 'road' that cut through the west side of the forest went on for at least a mile-and-a-half, leading to the Beasley residence. Walking that did not seem pleasant in the current situation. On the other hand, everything around here was considered evidence at this point, and on top of that, it simply wasn't Jake's to take. Or anybody's.

He looked at the Chief for guidance, but Walter was inspecting the woods for additional remains.

"Walter? What do we do?"

Walter looked at the blood in the dirt, then back at the Deputy. "Let's head back. We can barely get a radio signal out here anyway. Let's go before it gets too dark."

"Sounds good to me," Christine said. She walked with Shane passed Robert, who waited a moment, irritated with the recent conversation he had with Jake that literally announced his feelings for Christine. Those emotions were pale in comparison to the dread he was feeling. Like everyone else, he knew something was seriously wrong, that someone or *something* was in these woods, and he wanted nothing to do with it. He turned around and followed them to the house.

Walter gave one last look at the remains. The blood was still red. This kill was recent, the perpetrator likely nearby. He stood up to leave, only to turn on his heel at the sound of scurrying feet. A squirrel and two jackrabbits were taking off to the south, passing within inches of his feet.

There were more crackling branches to his right. More scurrying animals, all running and hiding in deep burrows.

As though retreating from a predator.

Jake was growing increasingly agitated as he stepped inside. He checked the desk drawers, the bedroom dresser, the kitchen area. No sign of any keys.

"Oh, this can't be happening," he said. He went into the living room area and started looking near the entertainment system.

Shane stepped inside.

"Hey, man, let us do it. This is a crime scene and you're getting your prints everywhere."

"No offense, Officer, but I'm not really concerned with that. I just wanna get the hell out of here, and fast."

"Let's just hotwire it," Robert said. Jake stopped, then turned around, feeling somewhat relieved to hear those words.

"I'm good with that...though I've never hotwired a vehicle before. Do you know how?"

Robert bit his lip. "I don't." Both men looked at Shane. They didn't speak the question, but he heard it as though they did. *Can you?* He looked out the window at the vehicle. It was a very old, though well-maintained vehicle. Probably pre-dating 2004. Probably wouldn't have been built with a fob which would be required for ignition.

"Probably." He stepped outside and walked to the truck.

"So, what's the plan?" Russ asked. "Take off together in this truck and wait for the State to arrive?"

"That's what the Chief said," Shane replied.

"Where is he?" Christine said.

"He's over..." Shane looked down the tree line toward the cow pasture, narrowing his gaze on the section of trees where they found the arm. He glanced around, seeing Christine, Russ, Ed, Beau...but no Walter. "He *was* over there." He looked around again, certain his eyes were playing tricks on him. "I thought he was following us back into the house." He hurried back through the front entrance, where Robert and Jake were standing. "Is the Chief in here with you guys?"

"I don't see him," Robert said, glancing about. Jake hurried into the kitchen and bathroom areas, looked back at Shane, and shook his head.

Back outside, Shane hurried around the back of the house. Walter was not near the pens, nor was he near the barn. *Was he checking inside again, perhaps?*

"Walter?" he called out.

"Chief?" Christine shouted. There was no reply. They sprinted to the barn, checked inside, and confirmed he was not there. "Where the hell is he?" Now, the other officers and hunters were concerned. They branched out across the farm, calling for the Chief.

Shane tried the radio. "Unit one, what's your location?" There was no answer. "Chief, come in please." Still, no answer. He looked over at his fellow officers and raised his speaker. *Your radios are picking up the transmission, right?* They nodded, understanding his gesture.

If they were picking up his frequency, Walter's radio should've been too.

They walked to the edge of the trees where they last saw him.

"Walter?"

They peered between two maples. The arm wasn't there anymore. Shane looked around, thinking he had the wrong spot.

But the claw marks were there. The blood...

"Were those prints there before?" Christine asked, pointing a few feet past the arm. They were the same as the ones they saw near the house. Huge; human; but yet, not human.

"Turn your radio volume down," Shane instructed. All the cops twisted their knobs until their radios were off. He raised his mic. "Walter? Can you hear us?"

"Down there," Christine said, pointing further back into the woods.

"I heard it too," Beau whispered.

Shane tried again. "Walter? You there?" They could hear the radio transmission echo from somewhere back there.

The group slowly pressed on. Branches swayed in the breeze, each movement causing a new chill down their spines. It was just dark enough in this forest for Shane to require his flashlight. He panned the white stream back and forth.

"Chief?"

He heard his own voice echo from just a few meters ahead. There were more of those prints in the dirt. They could see that the leaves here were crushed and shredded, as though someone had been stomping them around with their boots.

In the middle of it all was a radio. Walter Eastman's radio. Christine picked it up, stared at it, then looked into the dark woods.

"Walter?!"

"Guys?" Jake said, cupping his mouth. He was standing a couple of yards to the right, looking down. Shane walked over to see what he was looking at, and realized it was Walter's Glock lying in the leaves. It was unfired.

When Shane stood up, he realized that Jake was looking increasingly pale. His eyes were wide now, staring straight ahead, his hand still cupped over his mouth. Shane followed his gaze, then saw the bright red splattering on the middle of a tree trunk.

"Oh…my God."

There was something hanging from the bark; something loose, flappy, and wet. Dangling from *that* item were thin strands, caked in fresh blood. Though he didn't want to, Shane directed his light on it.

It was a piece of scalp, with grey hair, scraped against the tree.

CHAPTER 11

"Jesus Christ, man! What are we going to do?" Russ Linn said. The youngest member of the group was so on edge, it was making the others look emotionless in comparison. He paced back and forth in the Beasleys' backyard, not daring to look back into the woods.

"Russ, for godsake, I need you to pull yourself together," Shane replied. He was attempting to get back on the radio to Dispatch. "Dispatch, you read me?"

"I hear you now, Unit Two."

"Call the State Police and tell them to get up here quick. They need to make this a priority. The Chief's missing."

There was a pause.

"I'll get back on the phone with them."

"Holy shit, why the hell is it taking them so long?" Robert asked.

"The nearest trooper station is over an hour from here," Christine said. She spoke low, considering the adrenaline she was feeling, it was the only way she could speak clearly at the moment. "The Troopers were either busy elsewhere, or didn't even consider the call a priority at first."

"That, and they're probably trying to figure out how to find this place," Shane said.

"Fucking great," Beau said.

"So, what do we do?" Ed asked. They were all looking at Shane, who was now regretting his decision to accept his promotion. He was now the leading rank.

"Should we leave?" Russ asked.

"We can't just abandon Walter," Beau said.

"You think he's still alive?" Jake asked.

"There's no proof that he's not," Christine said. She looked at Shane. "*You* have to make the call, *Sergeant.*"

It was the first time he did not enjoy hearing her refer to him by the new rank.

His eyes were locked onto the thick forest. The trees were looking more and more possessed as night began casting its ominous shadow over them. Shane's mind shuffled through different phases of thought. There was the self-pitying stage of 'why me' and 'I'm never gonna work in an isolated town ever again'. After that ran its course, there was the sense of duty, and the thought of consequence. There was no worse thought right now than stepping into those woods in the dark.

But Walter was in there somewhere, and with no ETA on the State, Shane and his fellow officers were the only ones who could help him—if he was still alive. And that was the worst part; not knowing if he was alive.

"I'm going after him," Shane answered.

"You sure you want to do that?" Russ asked.

"I'm not gonna make anyone follow me," Shane said.

"I'll go," Christine immediately said. Even with her feelings for Shane, she was surprised at herself for speaking so quickly. Those woods were the last place she wanted to be.

Robert grinded his teeth, watching her gaze at her new boyfriend.

This prick's going to get her killed.

"I'll go too," he said.

"Me too," Beau said, raising his hand. Slowly, Ed Flowers raised his hand. Then, after some hesitation, Russ Linn raised his hand as well.

Shane nodded at the officers, then looked over at Robert.

"I appreciate your willingness to help, but I'd like you to stay here."

Robert's gaze turned fiery. "What?!"

"We don't know what we're walking into out there, and I don't want to take civilians willingly into harm's way," Shane explained.

"Oh, bullshit," Robert said.

"You're not coming. Simple as that," Shane said, his tone harsher. Robert opened his mouth to speak, but held back. Retaliating with a barrage of explicative language would not win him this argument and he knew it.

"You expect us to stay *here?*" Jake said, gesturing with his shotgun at the ravaged goat and pig pens.

"You're safer here than you'll be out there," Shane said.

"Really?!" Jake retorted, again gesturing at the damage.

"Wonder how that fared for the Beasleys," Robert added.

"You're *not* coming. Get it through your skull," Shane said.

"Robert, shut the fuck up," Christine said. Robert looked at her, then back at Shane. He scoffed, then performed a mock salute.

"Aye-aye, Sergeant."

"This is crazy," Jake said.

"If you can find the keys to that truck, you've got my permission to head into town. However, if you're gonna stay..." Shane looked over at Christine, "Mind handing them your radio?"

She took it off her belt then handed it to Jake.

"If the State shows up, or if you see or hear anything suspicious, radio us immediately," Shane instructed.

"You sure you'll even be able to find your way in there?" Robert asked.

"That's the advantage of being near the lake," Shane replied. He then pointed at the radio, "Make sure the volume is up high on that thing. Even if the signal is bad, the red light will turn green if it picks up an incoming transmission. You good?"

Jake glared at Robert for a second. *I'm pretty much stuck here because of you, you prick.* "Yeah, I'm good. Though if I see someone come out of those woods that isn't you, I'm not gonna ask questions. I'm gonna start shooting."

Shane closed his eyes. *Damn, Walter, for letting these guys tag along.*

"*Only* if you feel threatened," Shane replied. "Don't be shooting anyone else that might be lost in these woods."

"Not that many people here, Sarge. You said so yourself," Robert said. Shane chose not to continue the verbal sparring. Instead, he glanced at his fellow officers, all of whom were ready with their flashlights and sidearms.

"Alright. Watch your spacing while in there. Don't get too tight, but DEFINITELY don't branch out far. For godsake, keep an eye on the person next to you. Anyone sees anything, you let the rest of us know. We're all gonna be on the same page out here. Understood?"

"Yes, sir," Christine said, a phrase the other officers repeated. Shane took a deep breath, faced the woods, and pointed his light.

"Alright...let's go." He took the first step in, and was followed closely by the others.

Robert begrudgingly waited, watching Christine trek into the woods until she disappeared into the black. After a few yards, all he could see of them were the white streams emitting from their flashlights panning back and forth.

You better not get her hurt. Or worse.

CHAPTER 12

Rosie City.

It wasn't really a city as much as it was a town. Regardless, it was considered the busiest town for miles, though still incredibly meager in comparison to urban areas even in the same state. Still, every so often, State Trooper Sergeant Elijah Letson was able to find some degree of activity to keep him busy through the night.

He had been tracking the young man, Simon Cordle, for a week now. A traffic stop which resulted in an arrest for cocaine possession made Elijah aware that someone was funneling drugs into the county. There had been a couple of shootings in the recent past, one of which involved the seemingly innocent man, Simon Cordle. Even when investigating the scene, did Elijah find the random drive-by odd. Such occurrences were not common in the state, and if they were, they were done with a purpose. Not random violence.

Cordle's record wasn't the most serious he'd seen. Possession for marijuana at age seventeen. Two speeding tickets. No felonies. Not the worst candidate for a drug shipper, until he pissed off one of his customers. However, Mr. Cordle must've stayed in business, because as the Sergeant found out in his tales, the tenacious young man was traveling back and forth from the Boothbay Shipyard in Maine, where cargo crews were delivering drugs from Florida and foreign countries.

Elijah's private investigation came to a close, and with the help of three other troopers and the Piscataquis County Sheriff's Department, Simon Cordle was arrested, as were the buyers he was meeting with.

"No, no, no!" the panicking supplier said as he was pushed into the back of a squad car. "This is a misunderstanding. Please, don't!"

Elijah chuckled. He stood, arms crossed, the sleeves hugging the arms they covered, which were as muscular as Greek statues. He scratched the two-day beard he had grown, as he hated shaving. The women who preferred the full growth might've had an effect on that mindset.

Mr. Cordle continued his plea. "Officer, I promise, this is a misunderstanding!"

"No, this is two pounds of cocaine," Elijah repeated. "And probably five years for you. Relax, you'll probably only serve two." He slammed the door, muffling Cordle's tear-filled pleas.

He watched as the rest of the suspects were loaded into a wagon. Two troopers secured the door, then proceeded to climb into the seats. The driver glanced back at his superior.

"Sarge, Dispatch has been trying to get ahold of you."

"Nice of you to say something sooner," Elijah said. He turned the volume up on his radio and walked over to his own patrol car. "Car Five here. Go ahead, Dispatch."

"We've received another call."

"The missing person in Oak Grave?" Elijah said.

"That's affirmative."

He rolled his eyes. *Apparently, those small town cops up there can't handle anything themselves.*

"What's the update?"

"Sergeant, it's actually sounding quite serious. They're reporting several missing persons, possible homicides, and are now even stating that one of their own has gone missing."

"Holy shit. It sounds real!"

Elijah looked over his shoulder to look back at Trooper Alex McDermott. He was only a few years younger, but was barely mature enough for the troopers. Whenever the guy wasn't on the job, he was in his gym practicing MMA, and even admitted to wanting to hone his skills with some perps on the job. During his brief stint in Corrections he tried that, but in the prisons, it was rarely an instance of one-on-one fighting—something he found out the hard way. He figured his odds were better on the streets, hence he joined the troopers. More than once, Elijah reminded him that he picked the wrong state, and that he should've chosen some place closer to New York if he wanted high adrenaline action.

Alex had already expressed his disappointment that he didn't get to wrestle any drug dealers to the pavement. With the news of potential action taking place up in Oak Grove, he was eager to try his luck there.

"Don't look so excited," Elijah told him.

"Me? Never," Alex said, holding his hands out like 'whatever'.

"Dispatch? You sure there's nobody closer that can handle it?"

"Not anyone with jurisdiction."

"Oh, for Chrissake," Elijah muttered. "What about the County?"

"What *about* the County?" Deputy Rickenburg said.

"Don't you guys have any deputies in that region?" Elijah said.

"Hell no. That area's nothing but a maze of dense forest, rivers, and lakes. It's gonna take us forever to get over there. Especially at night," Rickenburg said.

"Hence they have their own police unit," said a short, deep-voiced Deputy, ironically named Page. It was a name that earned him plenty of jokes from his fellow Deputies.

"No shit," Elijah said. He groaned. He had received the initial call, but wasn't keen on making the trip. As far as he was concerned, there was a reason that town had its own police force. He figured that by the time he'd get there, they would've found the missing person themselves, which would've meant he wasted his time. Plus, there was the hope that the County would take care of it. Besides, he had other things he wanted to take care of.

Unfortunately, it appeared that the Oak Grave cops weren't crying wolf this time. Elijah gave a final glance at the squad car as it carried Simon Cordle away.

"Alright, Dispatch, I guess the report writing can wait. Anyone else eager to come along?"

"Hey, if it passes the time," Rickenburg said.

"I'll tag along as well. Won't hurt to see a little bit of countryside," said Page.

"Mind if I ride with you, Sarge?" Alex asked.

"Fine," Elijah said. "Alright ladies, if anyone needs to go pee, go do it now. God knows how long this'll take. It'll be harder to find this place than Page's dick."

"Must be a big, flamboyant town," Page bantered back, flipping the bird. The Troopers chuckled then doubled up into their vehicles. Elijah checked the search engine for Oak Grave. Luckily, the map had been updated in the past couple of years, allowing him to actually find it.

"You think we'll find anything interesting up there?"

"Just a tiny police department with some officers who don't know their asses from a hole in the ground," Elijah replied. He punched the accelerator and drove north toward Oak Grave.

CHAPTER 13

The temperature had dropped eight degrees, but it felt like twenty. Yet, Shane Alter was sweating. The tad of arthritis in his left knee was acting up as though he was a decade older, and never once did his heart resume a normal rhythm. He focused on his breathing, never letting it get out of hand, despite the natural urge to hyperventilate and panic.

He was at the front of the group. He kept his pistol holstered, but his hand resting firmly on it. He had it drawn at first, but he couldn't hide the tremors in his grip. Such a sight did not inspire confidence in his fellow officers, whom he was certain were just as nervous, if not more so, than him.

An owl hooted somewhere beyond the reach of his light. It worsened the feeling that they were being watched. Leaves flapped into view, carried by the breeze across the ground like tumbleweeds.

Christine was right beside him. Her weapon was drawn and pointed to the ground. It was not a display of confidence, however. She had to keep checking her grip to make sure her finger wasn't on the trigger. Like Shane, she couldn't rid herself of the jitters, but unlike him, she wasn't worried about appearances. She simply didn't trust whatever it was these woods were hiding.

Russ was regretting eating that hot dog he had stuffed down before riding out here. He never would have predicted this case would've gone this far. He certainly could never have predicted that Walter Eastman, by far the most experienced cop in their small department, would mysteriously go missing.

His shoulder was continuously bumped by Ed Flowers, who was making a constant effort to remain in the center of the group.

Why did I take this job in the middle of nowhere?

The answer was simple: because he liked the low-stress and tiny population. In fact, he loved the forest, which he found beautiful. Until now. Now, it might as well have been a gravesite. A Valley of the Shadow of Death. Every step was weighing on his soul.

Beau Stevenson was lagging behind by a few steps. He wished he remained behind, not out of a neglect of duty or lack of care for the Chief, but because of his knees. This was probably the most movement he performed in a month, and he was feeling it.

Not one of them wanted to be here. Had it not been for their respect for Walter, they wouldn't be. However, it was a struggle to maintain that motivation. There was a lingering feeling of eventuality that weighed down on some of the officers; an eventuality that they would find the killer. An eventuality that they would find Walter, or parts of him.

They were at a point of calling the 'who' that was out there a 'what'. No human could cause that kind of damage without leaving a trace of an instrument, such as a sledgehammer, machete, or a chainsaw.

Shane couldn't see any tracks. There were too many leaves on the ground, some old, some fresh, and with the wind carrying them about, they couldn't see any markings. They had been going in a straight line for a while now. Shane kept glancing at the moon for a sense of direction, but there were too many trees in the way. Considering their slow pace, they couldn't have gone for more than a mile and a half.

"Alter," Russ said. "Let's be honest here; this is like trying to find a flea on an elephant's ass."

"We know they went off in this general direction," Shane replied.

"Yeah, but that doesn't mean they went this way the entire time," Ed added. "They could have taken a right or left. Hell, maybe even be right behind us for all we know."

"Perhaps we should wait for the State," Russ said.

"You guys seem awfully happy to let them do our job for us," Christine said.

"Get a grip, lady," Ed said. "Nobody wants to find the Chief alive more than me. But get some common sense. We have everything working against us out here. No light. Almost no radio communication. No idea of who we're hunting."

"If it's even a 'who'," Russ added. Ed shone his flashlight at the surrounding woods. His face wrinkled tensely and he started shaking his head.

"Frankly, guys, I can't stand this. I think we ought to head back."

"I disagree," Christine said.

"Then *you* can keep looking. I'm heading back." Ed turned around and started walking.

"You serious?" Christine said.

"Hey, your boyfriend said himself that he wasn't ordering us to stay out here," Ed retorted. "Hey, I walked out here for well over a mile. I'll even come back out when we have more people around. And better equipment."

"You sure if you wanna go by yourself?" Shane said. Christine looked at him questioningly. *You're not going to stop him?* He leaned in. "He's no use if he's gonna be like this."

"Anyone coming along?" Ed said to the group. His attempt at an authoritative voice came out as shaky. Russ gnawed on his lip, gave one last look at the swaying branches up ahead, then turned to his right.

"I'm heading back too."

Ed breathed a sigh of relief. "Smart man. What about you, Beau?"

"Uh?" The overweight officer felt at odds. On one hand, he wanted to be back at the open ranch, but only because his knees were screaming at him. Not to mention the anxiety was causing a bad pressure in his lower back. "I'll stay."

"Fine. See you back at the ranch," Ed said.

Shane watched them walk off. "You do realize you're going east, right?" The two officers stopped. Shane pointed back with his right arm. "That's southeast, where you want to go."

"Yeah, I'm fine with following the shoreline," Ed said. The duo continued to walk into the darkness.

Once again, Christine got in Shane's face, hers clearly expressing her disapproval. "You seriously letting us split up?"

"I can't *make* them stay," Shane replied.

"Yes, you CAN!" she replied. "What? Did you take the promotion just for the extra bucks?"

"Yes, actually," Shane admitted. Christine felt disgusted at his answer.

"Well, I guess I learned something new about you."

"Give me a break!" he said in a sharp whisper. "Walter's gone, maybe dead, and you're worried about THIS?!" He waved a finger between himself and her.

Beau cleared his throat. Suddenly, he was wishing he doubled back with the guys. He waited while the two of them argued, panning his light through the trees. He passed left to right, seeing pines, a few elm trees, a red maple, with several bushes in-between them. He swung the beam of white illumination to the northwest at a small but tight grouping of pines. He started moving it further right, then aimed it right back at the pines suddenly.

"Huh?"

He swore he saw a reflection, like those he saw in the eyes of a deer when it stood on the road in front of his truck one late night. He remembered how, after it finally walked around the bend, how its eyes still captured the beam of light when it looked back at him.

Those were the same reflections he saw between the pines. At least, he *thought* he saw them.

No, it wasn't a mistake. I definitely saw them. He tried to convince himself it was probably a deer, a racoon, or a bird. Probably one of the latter, unless the deer in these woods stood eight or nine feet high. Then again, he remembered them being bigger, like the reflections in the eyes of a giant.

Whatever they were, they weren't there anymore. Beau turned the light back and forth, each time more frantic than the last.

"Whoa! Whoa!" Shane said, seeing the officer's unnerved motions. He put a hand over Beau's right arm. "What is it? What did you see?"

"There's—" Beau was worried he'd come off as crazy. It only took a couple of moments to overcome that worry. *Fuck it. Let them think it.* "There's something out there, Alter. I saw it. There's something..."

"Shh, shh," Shane whispered. "Where?"

"Behind those pines," Beau whispered back, thrusting his flashlight at the grouping of trees. Shane looked. They were fifty yards away at least.

Could he really have seen anything? Asking that out loud would only spark an argument. *Might as well check it out.*

He unholstered his Glock and inched forward, nodding at Christine to take the left. Beau hesitated, but then followed, making sure to keep close with Shane. He kept his eyes fixed on those trees. Shane held his flashlight in a reverse grip and held it across his chest, aiming his Glock over it. The pines grew larger and more menacing as they approached.

Gradually, they drew near. Within twenty feet, they began to circle around.

"Watch the front," Shane whispered to Christine. She could barely hear him. She held position, while the other two circled around the back of the grouping.

Leaves fell and branches cracked together overhead. Both men gasped and aimed their lights upward. Two squirrels, hopping between branches on a neighboring maple tree, carrying nuts and other prizes away.

"Fuck," Shane muttered. He panned his light down. Gritting teeth, he finished circling back, and finally he emerged with a half-frightened shriek.

Nothing. He panned his light back and forth. There was nothing behind the pines. The tension released in a sharp breath. Shane felt frustration and relief all at once.

Christine came around the other side.

"Maybe we should head back," Shane said.

"Huh?" Christine muttered.

"The forest is playing tricks on us," Shane said. "We're at the point of chasing ghosts."

"I saw it!" Beau said. He beamed his flashlight further north at the army of trees. "It could be anywhere."

"What *did* you see?" Christine asked.

"Eyes. I saw its eyes," Beau muttered. Shane and Christine looked at each other. Even she didn't know what to say. She had assumed that he saw something run behind the pines. But Beau's voice and body language didn't lie. He definitely thought he saw something that put him on edge. Then again, this entire forest was putting everyone on edge.

"I don't see anything," Shane said.

"No shit, it could be anywhere. There's hills, trees, rocks," Beau replied.

"And no Walter," Christine said.

After shining his light for several yards, Shane lowered it to the ground where they stood. Several pine needles were sprinkled over the leaves. He stared at it for a moment, finding it odd that the needles were in one concentrated spot, as though something had brushed a single branch of the tree. As he looked at it, the wind kicked up. The pine needles scattered like moths and were swallowed by the carpet of leaves they rested on.

They had been knocked free recently.

"Something wrong?" Christine asked.

"I…I don't—"

A high-pitched holler echoed from the east. It was a man's scream, by the tone of his voice, a younger man. Russ Linn.

All three officers spun on their heels, hurried back around the pines, and looked. There were more stammering sounds; words they could not make out due to distance and wind.

Christine focused her gaze on the direction where Russ and Ed walked off. There was a flashlight, buzzing low to the ground like a firefly, with another swaying above it.

The officers ran, with Beau struggling to keep up.

"Ed! Russ! What's going on?" Shane called out. He yelped as his foot caught a root. He spun like a dancer, miraculously keeping his balance, then continued closing the distance. The flashlights took greater form, and after a dozen more steps, they could see the figures in the dark that were Russ and Ed.

"What happened?!" Shane asked.

Both men were catching their breath, looking to the south. Ed was standing up, slightly hunched as though he had finished a hundred yard sprint, and Russ was on his back. Judging by the way he sat, and the path he made in the leaves, he had fallen down, then scurried backward with his elbows and feet. Both men pointed past that little trail of scattered leaves. Their lights landed on a black bulge in the ground.

It had no outright shape. At first glance, Shane would have described it as some sort of blob. It wasn't a mound. In fact, it wasn't even part of the earth. A closer inspection revealed fur all over the body.

"A bear," he said.

"If you can call it a bear," Ed muttered, his eyes still wide with shock.

"The hell happened to it?" Christine said. The bear's body looked like a saggy piece of meat with no skeletal structure to hold it together. The skull was flattened, looking like a pancake with red jelly coming out the eyes and ears. Only the snout maintained its shape.

"Looks like somebody took a giant mallet to it and beat it down like a porkchop," Beau said.

"This isn't right," Ed said. "No person can do this to a bear. Look at that thing, it's at least three-hundred pounds."

Christine walked around the other side. She stopped and gasped as numerous critters took off running, thinking the humans to be larger scavengers intending to take their slice of the remains. Most of them disappeared after a moment, with the exception of a turkey opossum that scampered from the bear's arm.

Her light revealed rib bones protruding through the flesh like stakes. The skin near the limbs was wrinkled and folded, like how a glove bunches up at the wrists. This thing had not been killed for food. This was an act of hatred. Vengeance. Perhaps it attacked another animal, who proceeded to stomp it into the earth in retaliation? What would mash a bear with such ease?

Ants and flies had already taken claim to the corpse, feasting on the open wounds. She aimed her light at the paw, which was angled back from the wrist at a forty-five-degree angle, teetering on the points of a broken bone. The paw itself was face-up and caked with blood. She leaned in to look at the nails. There were hairs wedged between them, more brown than black.

Shane stepped alongside her, studied what she was staring at.

"I think we have a clue to our suspect," he said.

"What has fur like this? A moose?" Christine asked.

"I doubt it," Shane answered. He glanced back at the sound of rustling leaves. It was just the opossum stumbling about. The thing was dragging its hind legs. Probably sick. Shane couldn't have cared less, as long as it wasn't anything sneaking up on them.

He turned his eyes back to the bear. "Whatever happened here, we missed it by maybe a day. The initial stages of decay have begun. Clearly, this thing has been here long enough for every critter in the forest to get a bite out of it."

"Can we go now?" Russ asked.

"We were *already* going," Ed remarked.

"Get a grip," Shane said.

"You're not seriously telling me this is in any way natural," Ed hissed. He was pacing back and forth. He looked past Shane, then pointed his light at the opossum. "And what the hell's wrong with that thing?"

They looked back at the scavenger. It was on its side, its chest, shoulders, and ribcage very clearly extended. It was kicking its feet and writhing.

"Bad meat?"

"Not important," Shane declared.

"Dude, something's up," Ed said.

"You think I don't know that?" Shane replied. He took a deep breath, counted to five, then looked Ed in the eye. "I'm not gonna tell you again. Keep it together, man." He glanced back at Christine, then back at Ed and Russ. "No more wandering off. Stick together."

"You're not expecting us to stay out here, are ya?" Ed asked, his eyes never leaving the corpse.

"No. We're heading back. Let's travel by the lake, and follow the shore back to the south edge. From there, we'll just have a small chunk of forest to cut through before we get back to the ranch. Everyone on the same page?"

Everyone nodded except Christine.

"What about the Chief?"

"We'll come back for him," Shane said. "Fact is, we're not gonna find him. We need the State and hopefully the County if they can get their asses over here."

"Well, I'm not wasting anymore time staying here," Russ said. He was the first one to start moving. The others followed. Christine and Shane gave one last look into the southwest. Another owl hooted.

That feeling of being watched returned.

"Come on," Shane said. He squeezed her hand. It took her a moment, but then she returned the gesture. Together, they followed the others toward the lake.

CHAPTER 14

Jake Cobbs couldn't take his eyes off the goat pen as he paced back and forth along the yard. He spent the few remaining minutes of daylight searching for the truck keys with no success. The power was out, and somehow, staying in that dark house was worse than being outside. He resigned himself to the likelihood that the keys were probably on Mr. Beasley's person when he disappeared, and decided to wait in the yard, where Robert happened to be waiting. At least here, they could run in any direction if they saw anything.

The downside was, they were surrounded by death. There were too many clouds covering the halfmoon, severely dimming the silver light it would supply. The trees were in constant movement thanks to that damn breeze. Jake was getting increasingly tense and frustrated. It was as though all of nature was conspiring to break his psyche.

The broken pens drew his gaze like magnets. No matter how much he wanted to look away, he wasn't successful for long. His mind would not do away with the question:

"What the hell happened to the goats?" he said it out loud. Robert was shining his flashlight around the trees, then back at him.

"Probably ran off."

Jake shook his head. He wanted to believe it, but that answer didn't make sense.

"Where are the bodies?"

"Whose bodies?"

"The farmers? What happened to the arm?"

"You're just now asking this?"

"I'm just now voicing it," Jake snarled. Robert could tell his buddy was gradually losing his cool. This was the exact reason why he did not want to be left stranded in the cabin in the middle of nowhere.

"Just hang tight," Robert calmly said. Being reassuring was not his forte, but he was self-aware enough to know that tough-love was not going to help the situation. "We'll be out of this...probably within the next couple of hours. Who knows? Maybe we'll get paid to be part of some documentary about this. From what I hear, those murder shows make bank."

The word *murder* had the opposite effect. It also didn't help that Jake was not a fan of those documentaries. And the possibility of money failed to ease his tension.

"I just want to get the hell out of here." He looked at his watch, which he could barely read in the dark. "How long has it been?"

"Half-hour, maybe."

There was no radio traffic. No sound. Nothing to indicate they were coming back.

Jake finally looked away from the pens and into the woods. In a way, that was almost worse. It wasn't the trees, but the thought of who...or what...was lurking behind them.

"Those cops need to hurry up."

****

Normally water had a calming effect on Christine Huron. She would often sit by ponds or by the lake in her spare time. Even in winter, just seeing water with the ducks floating over it gifted her a sense of levity.

It didn't work this time.

When they arrived at the lakeshore, it just looked like a black abyss. In the night, the water looked like tar, even though

Christine knew it was clean. It was as though something had taken possession of the entire forest.

The five cops took a breather before continuing on. Russ and Ed were still visibly unnerved by what they had recently seen, on top of all the previous events leading up to it.

Shane put a hand on Christine's shoulder. "You alright?"

She nodded, put her hand on his, then forced a smile. "Yeah." They remained silent for a moment. "Sorry for going off on you before. I know you're doing the best you can. I can't say I'd be handling it any better."

"Don't apologize, babe," he replied. He raised his voice slightly to speak with the others. "Let's keep going. Farm's that way." He pointed to the right.

"We should probably let the hunters know we're coming," Ed said.

"Good point." Shane holstered his sidearm and grabbed his radio. "Robert? Jake? You guys there?" He waited a sec. *Damn fucking radios.* "Guys? You there?"

"We're here. Any luck out there?" It was Robert's voice.

"No luck. We're heading back to the farm. We'll be emerging on the south side from the lake. So, do me a favor and don't shoot us."

"Did you fi—" Static.

"Oh, for the love of God," Shane groaned. He took a step back to see if he could get a better signal. "Please repeat."

He felt a *whoosh* right by his head. It was a sensation like wind, but not. Rather, something hurtling THROUGH the wind. All five of them turned at the sound of a splash. It was big, caused by something heavy. It wasn't as though a fish jumped, unless it was fifteen pounds. And no fish in this lake weighed more than five pounds.

Shane's brain connected the dots. The *whoosh,* the splash...something was thrown. He turned around and aimed his flashlight into the woods.

Beau saw what he was doing and repeated the action, aiming his light further north. At first, there was nothing but seemingly infinite forest. His light found tree after tree, each as stationary as the other. He panned back, then froze.

Those reflections were there again. This time, they weren't peering from between the branches of a pine. They were in the space between two baren maples. Eyes, connected to an ominous silhouette.

Shane heard the *whoosh* of another heavy object being thrown. Instead of a splash, what followed was the *crack* of solid impact. The huge rock that was flung from the trees bounced off its target and rolled on the ground.

All eyes turned to Beau Stevenson as he collapsed to his knees, then fell backward. His face was pancaked into his skull, which was now cratered inward, leaking blood through the nose, mouth, and deflated eyes.

Christine screamed, as did Russ.

"Oh God!"

Shane whipped his light back into the woods and saw the figure.

"THERE!" He drew his Glock and fired several shots. Ed was next to shoot, though he only caught a glimpse of the silhouette as it ran into the forest.

"Where'd he go?!"

"We can't stay here. We gotta go," Shane said.

"What about Beau?" Russ asked. The dead officer was not twitching. His collapsed face now served as a bowl for the blood that leaked.

"He's dead. We can't worry about him now. Let's go."

The radio started blaring. *"Hey?! What's going on? Did we hear gunshots?"*

"Standby," Shane replied. He lowered the radio then started north. "Come on, guys."

"We're leaving him here?"

"What do you want to do? Carry him back?" Shane replied. "He's dead. Let's get back to the farm."

Terror-stricken, the small band of cops followed their leader north, while keeping their lights pointed at the tree.

As he led them, Shane questioned what he saw. Was it a man? It was shaped like one, though it was nine feet tall at least. That rock that killed Beau, and nearly killed him, had been launched like a rocket for over a hundred feet, meaning its thrower had the strength of a gorilla.

The truth was evident. It wasn't a man lurking beyond those trees.

****

"Sergeant, goddamnit, what the hell's going on out there?!" Robert yelled.

"Wait up!" Jake called after his cousin as they ran along the fence to the north pasture. "Rob, they told us to wait!"

"The shots came from this way," Robert said. He lifted his radio again. "Christine? Where are you? You alright?!" There was no answer. *Jesus, she's in trouble.*

"Just stop, man," Jake said. They arrived at the northwest corner of the fence. Up ahead was a thin patch of trees between them and the lake corner. "They were supposed to be coming from this direction."

"Then, let's wait," Jake said.

Robert seethed, wanting to cooperate with Shane Alter's instructions, but overwhelmed by fear that something had happened to Christine. He looked into the woods, hoping to see flashlights coming through.

Jake was panting. His knees were killing him, though that agony was nothing compared to the anxiety-induced cramping in his stomach. He could barely grip his shotgun properly. He watched the trees as well as Robert's body language. He knew that if Robert went, he would follow. Partly out of loyalty, partly out of fear of being alone. So far, it looked like his cousin had just enough self-control to wait here for the cops.

Thank God.

****

Shane could see the bend in the shoreline a hundred feet ahead. Another fifty feet beyond that was the forest dividing them from the Beasley Ranch. All they needed to do was plunge through, get in that ranch, hotwire that truck, and get the hell out of dodge.

Christine was right behind him, running alongside Ed Flowers. Russ was at the back of the group, frantically gazing at the woods to their right. Thus, he didn't pay attention to the ground in front of him.

The small dip in the ground that the others were able to avoid caught him by surprise. It was only six inches, but for a man running full-speed, it might as well have been a cement ledge. Russ fell forward, his body reverberating upon impact. It wasn't the fall that alerted his fellow officers, but the discharge of his weapon, which launched a bullet aimlessly into the woods.

The others stopped and whipped around, then saw the younger officer floundering on the floor. They felt the initial fear that another rock had been thrown, only to realize it was simply the result of clumsiness and fright.

"Get up, Russ!" Shane said. He ran to the officer and lifted him to his feet.

****

Robert gasped. Another gunshot. New fear seized his mind. Something was happening. Christine was in danger.

Jake watched as his cousin stepped toward the woods, rifle poised at shoulder level.

"No, wait...fuck!"

He dashed into the woods behind Robert. A second later, they were surrounded by a world of trees. The patch of forest had every obstacle imaginable. They moved to the left to get around a couple of pine trees as wide as forklifts, only to nearly get entangled in thick bushes with branches that resembled spider legs.

Jake was now in the lead. He moved further left, getting around the obstacles in a tight semi-circle, then stepping left once again to avoid colliding into an elm tree. His sidestep only put him in the path of another obstacle. He figured it was another tree, until his light struck brown fur instead of bark. He saw broad shoulders, a hulking chest, and a disproportionally shaped head baring razor teeth like a deep-water fish.

Shrieking, Jake raised the shotgun, which was immediately snatched out of his hands by one of the arms. With hands thick as cement blocks, it bent the weapon as though it were a paperclip.

Then he screamed as those arms found him.

Robert had gotten turned around after his foot had gotten snagged in a root. He pulled himself free, then heard the screams. He turned to his left and saw Jake's flashlight fall from his grasp. He aimed his own, then froze. His cousin was clutched in the grasp of a humanoid thing. Its arms were thick as tree trunks. Its head protruded between the shoulders like a deformed mountain. He saw skin around the eyes, malformed from years of infection and endurance. One eye socket was significantly larger than the other. The body was covered in brown fur, except for areas covered in thick scabs.

It stood at nine feet, leveling Jake's face with its own. With Robert's flashlight now aimed at them, the hunter was forced to see the hideous details of his killer's identity, including the rotting left check, which had dissolved into a few strands of red tissue stretching over the jawline. Streams of saliva dripped through the side of its mouth. Hot breath touched his face.

Jake screamed, then felt cool wind embrace his body as the creature swung him like a baseball bat right into the trunk of a tree. His scream ended with a wet splattering sound, as his head exploded like a dropped egg. Skull and brain wet the soil at the monster's feet.

Now Robert was screaming. The beast turned and saw its new victim. Tossing its recent kill to the side, it advanced. Robert backtracked. Simple things became nearly impossible. His finger struggled to find its way into the trigger guard. His light wavered, hitting the beast as it closed in. Each step it took was equal to three of Robert's.

It had closed within six feet when Robert finally squeezed the trigger, firing from the hip. The aimless bullet managed to catch the beast in the right shoulder, jerking it to the side and briefly halting its advance. It touched the wound, smelled its own blood on its fingertips, then roared angrily at Robert.

The hunter cocked the lever to fire another shot. It struck the beast in its outstretched arm as it lunged for him. It didn't stop this time. Fingers, eight-inches long and thick as college textbooks, tore the rifle from his grasp, bent it out of proportion, then threw it into the woods. Those same hands then reached for him. At that moment, he saw the pointed, razor-sharp nails protruding from those fingertips. Screaming, he ran.

****

"Someone's screaming," Christine said. The cops dashed into the forest, having been spurred on by the sound of gunshots. Once they penetrated the forest, they heard the sound of a struggle. Then they saw a waving flashlight, held by a retreating man.

"This way," Shane said. His weapon was drawn again as he led the charge. The span of a few moments brought to view a horrified Robert Windle and the thing behind him. It reached forward and grabbed the hunter by the shoulder, the fingertips like scalpels, cutting deep into his skin. Robert yelled as it lifted him off the ground.

All four officers gasped.

"JESUS!" Ed shouted.

Now, it was real. It wasn't a man. Yet, it wasn't an animal. Shane could only describe it as a mixture of both. It was primordial, like something that history had tried to bury, yet somehow couldn't. A legend so untamed that it was known across the globe. Sasquatch; Wildman; Yeti…

Bigfoot.

The beast roared and closed its other hand on Robert's head, ready to twist it off like a bottlecap.

Shane aimed his Glock and fired. Bullets struck Bigfoot's ribcage, sparking pain and rage. The beast jolted from sudden pain, dropping its prize. Robert landed on his back, his arms sprawled out.

The other officers joined in. The beast turned to maneuver between the trees, but not before more bullets struck its left shoulder simultaneously. Blood spurted from the wound…all over Robert. He screamed at the warm sensation splattering on his face, chest, and shoulders. He rolled to his arms and legs, then crawled away in the opposite direction.

Flashlights whipped about. The beast had moved out of sight.

"Where is it?!" Russ asked.

They heard crackling branches behind them. They all turned and beamed their lights. There it was, thirty yards back. In its arms was a twelve-foot section of a branch. It threw the branch like a Scottish caber right into the group's center, forcing them to dash in separate directions, and effectively separating them.

Russ stumbled, fell to his knees, while fumbling to keep his weapon in his grasp. He had dropped his flashlight, leaving him draped in darkness.

"Where is it?!" he shouted, though all the others were several feet away from him. The earth trembled like a mighty drum was beating it, each beat was more intense than the last, until the beast emerged from the darkness.

Russ screamed as he was grabbed and lifted off the ground, drawing the attention of his companions. Their lights pointed his way from three separate directions, each in time for their owners to see Russ being raised high over Bigfoot's head. One hand held him by the shoulder, the other by the groin, and slowly, they bent him back like a horseshoe. Russ spasmed and screamed, which intensified at the snapping of his spine.

Christine screamed, seeing her colleague in a V-shape, pivoting in the center of his back. Bigfoot dropped the prize and ran for the scream.

"Christine! Look out!" Shane yelled. He sprinted toward his girlfriend, jumping over debris, only to stumble over Jake Cobb's headless body. He screamed upon seeing the stump, scampered on all fours, then redirected himself to continue toward Christine.

Bigfoot got there first.

She heard the cracking of twigs behind her. Gasping, she dove forward, narrowly avoiding his grasp. She turned around to shoot, only for her gun to be swatted from her grip. Unarmed, she stumbled backwards, eyes wide, and mouth agape to scream, but unable to get it out.

Bigfoot raised his arm to swing at her. Christine threw her arms over her head, consciously knowing it wouldn't be enough to keep herself from getting decapitated, but succumbing to natural instinct nonetheless.

Gunshots rang out. Bigfoot stumbled, his attack foiled by the male officer advancing from behind him.

Christine lowered her arms and saw the beast turning around. As he did, his arms swung at her, the knuckles connecting with her lower jaw. Not as hard as a deliberate attack, but still enough to knock her off her feet. She hit the ground hard, her head clunking against the root of a tree. She lay motionless on her back, hearing the sound of gunfire and roaring. Yet, she was powerless to do anything except stare straight upward. The forest was spinning behind blurred vision. Then, it faded to black.

Shane fired another shot into the advancing creature's chest. Despite the pain, it kept coming. Realizing it wasn't stopping, he spun on his heel and sprinted in the opposite direction.

More bullets whizzed by Bigfoot's head, until one finally grazed his brow. He turned to his left, baring teeth in anger at the other remaining human.

Ed Flowers squeezed the trigger several more times, but only twice did the gun discharge. The rest were hollow *clicks*. Despite hearing them, the adrenaline spurred him to keep 'shooting', even as the thing came at him. Like Shane, he turned to run, only to faceplant into a tree. He stumbled, then fell to his knees.

Grains of dirt leapt off the ground as huge footsteps reverberated underneath like shockwaves.

Ed felt the weight of the creature, literally, as it drove its heel into his back, flattening him to the ground. It planted its foot between his shoulder blades and pressed down. Ed squealed until all the breath was driven from his lungs. His spine popped, as did his upper ribs. Then came the intense pressure in his stomach, heart, lungs, and intestines.

All at once, they ruptured like grape tomatoes.

Shane reloaded his weapon and double-backed, but was too late. By the time he located the beast, its heel was pressed all the way to Ed's stomach...from behind. The officer's insides burst out of every orifice, leaving a limp, twitching corpse.

The beast already saw him. Wasting no time, it charged. Shane didn't bother shooting. For the second time, he sprinted. He weaved around several trees, hearing the thing gradually closing in behind him.

All of a sudden, he was on open land. He was on the Ranch. Dead ahead was the north perimeter fence line. Directly behind him was the Bigfoot, now sprinting without obstacle as well.

Shane went for the fence. Within three feet, he jumped as high as he could. He snagged briefly on the upper wires, but to his surprise, he flipped over gracefully. He landed on the ground in a summersault, then sprang to his feet, and continued running.

Bigfoot arrived at the fence. Enraged at its obstruction, it grabbed handfuls of metal wire and ripped them from their posts, turning the section of fence into a crumpled mesh. It passed through the empty space and ran after the officer.

Shane could hear it closing in. The intensity of its footsteps was like a gauge to measure distance, which was rapidly dwindling. All sense of reasoning was lost. He dropped his flashlight, as though that would somehow make him go faster. All it did was make him blind. Perhaps it was best not to be able to look into the decaying face of the beast. It was almost on top of him now.

He heard it roar, only a few steps behind him.

Then, all of a sudden, he experienced brief weightlessness, which ended in a sudden stop. Shane was coated in darkness. The smell of mud filled his nose. There were walls all around him, as though he was in some horrible esophagus. Moist dirt compacted in his fingertips.

The well—he had fallen into the well.

He looked up, barely able to see out the mouth of the newly dug well. The creature was stomping up there, uncertain why its victim had mysteriously disappeared.

It moved slowly, growling, keeping close to the well. It knelt at the edge, which was only a little wider than three feet. Shane could hear the grazing of an arm reaching down from the edge. He crouched as low as he could, then fumbled for his Glock, which he had dropped. He found the dirty weapon and clutched it tight.

The arm stopped within inches of his brow, grasping at air.

Terror resulted in clenched teeth and tight muscles, and a sheer willpower to not discharge the weapon. He wasn't sure if Bigfoot knew he was down here.

It did.

The beast considered its options. It couldn't see how deep the hole was. Even as accustomed to the dark as it was, even its eyes could not penetrate the pure blackness in that pit. It had not seen this hole during its previous attack on the farm, and until daylight, it had no way of knowing how deep it was. All it knew was that its prey was out of reach.

The options were to dig it out now, which would take time and energy—much of which had already been spent today. Or, it could return tomorrow. There was a pleasure in the thought of leaving the human to rot here, to die of starvation in his own grave. It seemed unlikely it would be able to climb out.

A gravely sound rolled in its throat; Bigfoot's version of laughter. It turned around, and without a second thought, it returned to the woods to collect its catch.

****

Robert Windle was on his hands and knees. His shoulder throbbed, though that pain was insignificant compared to the throbbing in his temples. Much of the pain was stress-induced. No person, save for some combat soldiers, were capable of bearing the sight of such mass death. His mind was still whirling around the fact that they had actually discovered a true-to-life Wildman in Oak Grove Forest. The legends were real, and the reality was so much worse than he ever could have imagined.

He could hear moaning from somewhere in the field of death. At least one of the officers was still alive.

Christine? He didn't see her go down. He glanced about at the carnage. Even with several dropped flashlights lighting the area of forest, it was hard to spot anything other than trees and bushes.

Ed Flowers' corpse was the nearest one, his shoulder blades cratered into his torso. Robert's stomach churned, seeing the blood spilled from the mouth, nose, and eyes like some demented Halloween decoration. He scampered away from the sight, then looked about to see if Christine was anywhere close. He trembled. Did he even want to see her? If she was crushed, or split apart, the sight of her would be a thousand times worse than seeing his cousin Jake Cobbs' headless corpse—an image that would haunt him forever. But if she was still alive…

He could hear the creature's footsteps at the edge of the forest. He had seen it take off to the south after Shane. There were no gunshots, just sounds of ripping and tearing.

It was walking now, in no hurry, meaning Shane was probably dead. He couldn't see it yet, but knew that would change in the span of a few short moments, during which he needed to find a place to hide. He crouched low, his buttocks in the air as he pushed himself backward. He glanced around frantically, his heart racing. Ultimately, he settled for a thick patch of thorn bushes. The thorns prodded his face and neck, drawing blood as he quietly forced his body in-between them.

From there, he remained motionless, and watched the forest directly ahead.

The monster appeared on the left, its body a mere silhouette. It had adapted to use the darkness to its advantage, as it had proven by ambushing the hunters and cops. It stopped for a moment then touched its hands to its shoulders and chest. It bellowed in pain at the touch of its bullet wounds. It nestled around, picking up sticks and twigs, bending each one to test its stability. Most snapped effortlessly. Only the ones that offered any resistance to its immense strength were kept.

Whatever injuries it sustained did not appear to be life-threatening, as its next course of action was to collect its bounty. It lumbered through the woods, its eyes pointed down, searching for the humans it had killed. It found Russ Linn's broken body first. It picked him up by the heels and flung him over its shoulder like a potato sack. Carrying its prize, it continued walking back and forth, eventually finding Jake Cobb. Blood trickled from the headless stump as Bigfoot slung him over its shoulder over Russ.

Robert heard a groan. He winced, a result of fright and empathy. Russ was still alive, though thoroughly paralyzed. Robert had suffered some minor back pain in his life which he healed through physical therapy. He remembered the debilitating pain, which was minor compared to what other patients were experiencing. Doctors always asked the 'from-one-to-ten' question regarding the scale of pain. He winced again. What Russ was experiencing had to be twenty.

Bigfoot turned around.

Robert froze, his empathy disappearing, making way for pure fright. The beast was now facing his direction. His body twitched uncontrollably, fighting the temptation to flee. It was walking in his general direction now, slightly to the left of him. At twenty feet, Bigfoot stopped, turned to its right, and found Ed's body. It tossed his body over the other victims on its shoulder, the impact generating a stomach-churning squelching sound.

It sniffed, turned, and looked around, as if it knew it had missed one of the humans it had encountered. Its eyes faced the bush.

Robert tightened every muscle in his body in an effort to control the nervous twitches. He watched through the branches, seeing the dark shape seemingly staring directly at him. Could it see him? Did it smell his blood? Each moment was a nightmare. He was unarmed, injured, and in close proximity to a killer that would snap him in half as easily as he would a matchstick.

He held his breath.

Finally, the beast turned and walked back where it came. After fifty feet it turned to the right, passing within the beam of a flashlight. It quickened its pace, walking through a dozen yards of dark forest before stepping into the beam of another dropped flashlight.

Robert watched as it knelt down and reached with its free arm, scooping up another body. The light revealed the strands of hair that dangled from its victim's head.

Christine! Robert wanted to scream. The beast tucked her under its arm, looked about one more time, then walked northwest until it disappeared into the darkness.

CHAPTER 15

For several minutes, Shane heard nothing except leaves being tossed about by the wind. He felt around him, still blinded by the darkness. He wanted to escape this dungeon, but was still paralyzed with fear. He heard the thing move away, but that didn't guarantee that it wasn't nearby. After all, it had proven to be stealthy when it needed to be. It had nabbed Walter without any of them knowing, and it had been keeping track of their movements without being heard. Clearly, it knew how to control its movements and use the forest to its advantage.

What if it was waiting nearby, just to ambush him once he escaped the pit?

Even so, there was something about being in this pit that was worse than that. It was like being in the belly of some giant beast. Adding to that misery were tingling sensations on his skin, followed by odd stings that made him jolt, as though hit by electric wire. After a few minutes, he felt all kinds of movement. Then it dawned on him: ANTS!

They were everywhere, crawling from pores in the dirt walls. This deep below the earth, they were protected from the cold temperatures above. And now, they had found a hundred-and-eighty-five pounds of meat to tide them through the winter. Normally, they would steer clear of the giant bipeds that roamed the forest. But here? Trapped in the dirt tunnel with nowhere to go? Shane Alter had practically rung the dinner bell.

He felt them crawling onto his hands and neck. Shane clawed at himself. Suddenly, the fear of being mashed to death under Bigfoot's fists felt like a luxury, compared to being slowly eaten alive. He jumped, raking his fingertips at the dirt walls. He felt the slightest hint of a ledge. His fingernails snagged briefly, but lost the grip. It was too narrow. He tried again and again, coating his hands with mud.

Tiny legs pricked at his nose and brow, the sensation quickly moving toward his eyes. He brushed his sleeves over his face then jumped again, grunting with each movement. A sting along his earlobe triggered a scream.

He was trapped, doomed to be stripped apart in a slow, excruciating manner.

"Hey!"

He looked up, only to cover his face again as a blinding light flooded the well. The light angled off, its reflections revealing the face of Robert Windle.

"Get me out of here, man!" Shane shouted up at him.

"Here," Robert replied. He lowered a branch, which Shane immediately grabbed. Like scaling a cliff, he pulled himself up, with the hunter tugging back on the branch as though it were a rope.

Solid ground and a cool breeze never felt as good as the moment Shane stepped out of the pit. He yanked his jacket off and shook it like a rug, then thew it down to allow his hands to continue brushing the critters off his face and body. He then pounded his chest and stomach like a gorilla to crush any ants that had gotten in his clothing.

After two minutes of hysterics, he finally calmed down. He looked over at the hunter, who stood with the dropped flashlight from one of the other officers. Shane looked to the ground, found the one he dropped during the chase, and picked it up.

"Thanks," he said to Robert.

"Lucky I heard you screaming in there. I figured you were dead too," Robert replied.

Images of the Bigfoot flashed in Shane's mind, causing him to look back into the forest. "Did you see where it went?"

Robert pointed northwest. "It took everybody. They're all dead. Scooped them all up like dead squirrels and carried them off." He winced as the recent memory replayed in his mind. "Jake, Ed, that young officer…"

"Russ," Shane said.

"I think he's still alive," Robert said. He inhaled, not wanting to state the last victim's name. But he had to. Not acknowledging it would only torment his mind further. "Christine."

"It took her?!"

"It picked her up last and carried her off with the others," Robert said. "She wasn't moving."

"Christine…I don't think she's dead," Shane replied. Robert whipped his gaze back at the officer.

"What?"

"I think she's only unconscious. I saw her go down. She took a hard hit, but I don't think it was fatal. You said it simply picked her up and carried her off? It didn't…" Shane hesitated… "finish her off, first?"

Robert grimaced. Shane could've put it more delicately, but all the same, he understood the point.

"No. Just reached down and grabbed her."

"It probably thinks she's dead. She's probably still alive!"

"Then I'm going after her," Robert said. Without saying another word, he marched into the forest, panning his flashlight along the ground for pistols. Shane hustled after him.

"Wait, we need a plan."

"Yeah. The plan is to follow its trail. It's bleeding. We'll have an easier time finding it."

"We need backup," Shane replied. He tapped his duty belt for his radio, only to realize it wasn't there. *Damn it. Must've dropped it in the pit or somewhere in these woods. Either way, I'll never find it.*

"If you were so keen on backup, you would've waited for it before," Robert said. His tone was accusatory, something Shane picked up on. He was divided on whether to call Robert out on it. After all, the guy literally just saved him from the pit.

"I don't—" Shane stammered. He wasn't sure on what to say.

"You knew you guys weren't equipped for a deep trek into the woods at night. And you went in, even after seeing what happened here at this ranch," Robert continued. "And now Christine's gone."

"Walter was gone, man," Shane replied. "We had to try and look for him."

"And now they're all dead. Except, maybe Christine. If only she stuck with me and didn't follow you, she wouldn't be in this mess. She—Agh!" Robert clenched his injured shoulder, then dropped to his knees. Shane rushed by his side.

"You alright, man?"

"Get off me," Robert replied, shaking Shane off of his other shoulder. The officer stepped back, not keen on agitating the hunter further. He assumed Robert was suffering a partial mental breakdown. This whole evening had been a stress overload, which boiled over into the recent slaughter which they narrowly survived. To make matters worse, they couldn't just walk away from it. Russ was still alive for sure, and so was Christine. At least, they hoped. Perhaps it was the uncertainty that was really breaking Robert's psyche.

The hunter took a breath, then stood back up.

"Sorry," he said. He walked around a little more, then finally found a Glock near a large puddle of blood. He started to reach for it, then withdrew his hand. It was Ed Flowers'. Finally, he snatched it, immediately shaking the blood off of it as fast as he could. Turns out, the weapon was useless, as the magazine was empty. He tossed it aside and walked to where Russ had gone down. It took a few minutes, but his light found the reflection from the metal slide. He picked it up, found that it had a nearly full mag, then held it tight with both hands.

He saw Shane kneeling near a tree. "She went down here." The officer panned his flashlight along the ground. "There's blood. Like you said, it was going northwest."

Robert approached him, then found Christine's Glock lying a few meters to the right. He picked it up, found another mag, mostly full. He ejected the loaded mag, transferred some of the bullets from Christine's, resulting in a fully loaded weapon with six bullets to spare. He tucked the extra mag in his pocket, then slammed the full one home.

It was clear Shane didn't need to offer him firearm training. The officer pointed at Robert's injured shoulder.

"You sure you don't want me to take a look at that first?"

Robert shook his head. "Let's stop wasting time. We need to find Christine." He aimed his light at the red droplets on the ground, located beside broken twigs and footprints. "That way. You coming?"

Shane hesitated. He knew they were outmatched. The thing had been shot numerous times, but only seemed to sustain mild injuries. Perhaps its muscular structure was so thick, it was like Kevlar. It could be hurt, but they needed high-powered rifles to do the trick—something they didn't have access to at the moment.

However, it was clear Robert was going no matter what. Additionally, Christine was probably alive, and one thing was for sure: they were her only hope.

He looked at his mud-caked weapon. It would take an hour to clean it properly, and that would be with appropriate gauze, tools, and oil. He took Christine's pistol and placed his magazine into that one. The chambering of the first round went smoothly, making him confident that the weapon wasn't damaged. He placed his own compromised weapon on the ground, then turned to face Robert.

"Alright, let's go," he said.

CHAPTER 16

Christine, in all of her years of hunting, was always curious about the experience of death. Not out of some gothic nature, or sadistic fascination, or even religious undertones. She, like most humans, had the underlying fear of death and wondered what happened to the mind once the brain shut down. Specifically, one's consciousness. Did the memory get wiped and the consciousness transferred to another being? Was there Heaven and Hell? Did such a thing exist? She never had any real religious leanings, usually considering herself more agnostic than anything else. However, she longed for something that many religious people had, which was a certainty of what happened to the soul, or what she simply thought of as consciousness. Even if Hell existed, at least she had an idea of what to look for, not that she wanted to be there. But she hated the unknown, probably because of what she really feared, which was nothingness. Specifically, the idea of being trapped in a world of eternal black, as though the eyes had shut permanently, and that would be all she'd ever see again.

Am I dead?

When her eyes opened, there was nothing but darkness. It was so thick, she couldn't see her hand in front of her face. She even questioned if she was even awake. She had never been covered in such darkness. The closest thing were underground cellars...

Underground...

Her brain registered the smell of dirt. She was suddenly aware she was lying face-down on the ground. Her jaw throbbed. Pain. Dead people don't feel pain. She tasted blood in her mouth. She wiggled her tongue, feeling the crown that was loosened when she was struck. Her senses were returning.

One sense might be a trick of the mind. Multiple senses: taste, smell, the feeling of movement—dead people don't do that. Still, she couldn't see. She lifted her head and looked around. She may as well have been blindfolded.

She curled her fingers, feeling dirt under her nails. Wherever she was, she way lying on the earth.

She extended her right arm, first dead ahead, then out to the side. She felt something like a wall. Not as hard as concrete along the surface, but somehow just as durable. She ran her hand around the wall, feeling grains of dirt flaking off. Was this a dirt mound? What was this? *Where* was this?

The next sense to return was her hearing. There was a scraping sound, as though something was rubbing against the dirt a few feet away. As she picked up new sounds, so did she pick up new smells, and suddenly, she was longing for the dull stench of dirt. There was a horrid stench coming from somewhere behind her, like rot. Whatever it was, it triggered the urge to vomit. Her weakened mind nearly succumbed to this urge, leading to a few dry-heaves. Perhaps there was nothing to cough up. She hadn't eaten anything in the last several hours, and only had a light lunch around noon.

The fact that she even remembered this was another reminder that she was indeed alive, not dead.

The next reminder was fear, triggered by a suction of air—a gasp for breath, which led to a dull moan. She froze. A second moan followed. It was barely audible, as though the source barely contained any life. Whatever it was, it was somewhere behind her.

She trembled uncontrollably, as though suffering from low blood-sugar. Her rapid heartbeat and the cramping in her stomach made it clear to her that wasn't the case. The silent terror she experienced eliminated any cravings...except for a cigarette.

A realization came to mind; the lighters in her pocket!

She reached into her pocket, pulled one of her lighters free, and ignited a flame.

A dancing orange light pierced the darkness, its glow coating the strange wall beside her. As she had thought, it was made of dirt, as was the ceiling above her. She looked to her left and saw another wall, exactly resembling the other. Decaying roots from trees and other flora poked through the walls, having died from failing to find a source of water here.

Panic slowly gripped her. The smells, the roots, the dirt all around her—she was underground.

Memories of the incident assaulted her mind. *It* had brought her here. For what? She didn't focus on that, as a more important question surfaced: Where was it? She glanced about, seeing no trace of its mass. A creature of that size in a relatively small tunnel such as this, there was no way it would be able to hide. She turned around and held her lighter out. The beast was not there. What was there, however, made her gasp loudly.

Right behind her was Ed Flowers' mangled corpse, lying face-up. His face and neck were bloated, the chest and stomach distended as though it had been pumped with air. The eyes were bulging from their sockets, the shoulders hunched forward and much broader than before. Lying beside him was a headless body. Only the lower jaw and tongue remained. Then there was Walter Eastman, who was killed in almost a similar fashion, though his skull was mostly intact, though just barely. His left eye-socket was completely deflated, as was the back of his skull. Much of his scalp was missing, and in the bit that remained was bits of bark from the tree he was repeatedly smashed against. And placed beside his body was Russ Linn, laying on his side, motionless, still partially bent backward in a V-shape.

Christine held back tears; a combination of sorrow and the fear that what happened to these men would happen to her next.

There was something else, but she couldn't make out what it was in the dim flame. She reached into her pocket and found her smartphone. The screen was heavily cracked, the battery at thirty-percent. No bars. She swept her thumb up along the lower screen and found the flashlight setting. A white stream engulfed the tomb. What she saw caused her temples to throb.

Beyond the bodies of her friends was a graveyard of slaughtered pigs, goats, deer, and coyotes, all lined up in organized rows.

Lightheadedness took its toll. She scurried backward, dropping her phone in the process. With the flashlight lying against the dirt and the screen powered down, she was once again shrouded in complete darkness. Still, she kept retreating, until the crack of a rigid object under her elbow caught her attention. Whatever it was, it was dry and narrow. Then there was something else with a similar sensation, but much larger.

Christine stopped and ignited a new flame from her lighter.

Empty eye sockets stared back at her, the white bone caked in years of dirt. Finally, she screamed and threw herself away from the skull. She took a few breaths, then leaned forward again. It took several additional moments to collect herself enough to inspect the find.

First, she used the flame to locate her dropped phone. Its white stream revealed worms burrowing their way out of the dirt walls as she panned back to the skeleton.

It was a cow skull, completely void of any meat. The term 'dry as a bone' had truly found its meaning here. This thing must have been dead for years. Decades, even. Christine was no biologist, but she remembered from school how it took years for nature to do its work on the dead. This thing was so old and so dry, that it cracked under relatively light pressure. Which made her wonder; how long had this thing been here? How long had this *creature* been here?

To the left was another skeleton. And another. Many had been stomped into the dirt. Looking further to the right, she saw more bones, mixed with a substance she didn't immediately recognize. It was dry and loose, not flesh, definitely not fluid—

Clothing!

Despite her reservations, she inspected the find. The remnants of what looked like an old denim jacket tore easily when she pulled it away, revealing the human skull under it.

"Oh Jesus! God!" she cried. Her instinctual reaction to scoot back caused her boot to bump the rest of the skeleton, what wasn't beaten into powder. All she could see was a leg with the shoe still attached to the foot, some pelvis and spinal column. No ribs, and maybe one arm. She didn't look too closely.

Something flopped out from the mound of rotted clothing that covered it. It was a black object, roughly three inches long and thick. Christine was ready to scream again, thinking it might be a large bug or spider feasting on any remains that might've been there. The light reflecting from coins spilled from the object snapped her into focus. A wallet.

Before going any further, the instinct of self-preservation kicked in again. She looked back and forth in the tunnel, making sure the beast was nowhere to be found. There was no sign of it, nor was there any indication of a way out. It had to exist, but where would she go? How far? And what if it came back?

She looked back at the skull, then at the wallet. She picked it up and opened it. Dirt and a few coins trickled out. She sorted through the cash inside, before finding an old, faded photograph of a young man and his parents. Then one of a pretty girl, roughly the age of nineteen.

Then she found the license. It was faded, though somewhat protected by the leather exterior of the wallet.

Joseph Finley Wheeler. Date of Birth: 04/24/1952

Christine read the data over and over again, then tried to convince herself that this had to be some sort of nightmare. But it wasn't. Those teens that disappeared in 1970, who were never found, she was looking at one of them right now.

This thing had been here since 1970? At least! Why hasn't anyone seen it?!

Within the next moment, she discarded the questions, as there were more important things to worry about. Common sense dictated that remaining here would simply result in not only death, but grave disappearance. She would *never* be found, except by future victims who had the luxury, or rather, *misfortune*, of being brought here alive.

She heard something behind her. She whipped around, her hand going for the pistol that was no longer in her holster. Tense, she peered into the tunnel. She heard it again, a low sound, like a mumble. A moan. She aimed the light at the corpses.

Russ Linn's arm moved. He was still alive!

"Oh God! Russ!" She hurried to his side, forcing herself not to look at Ed and Jake's horrifying corpses. In a way, seeing Russ was worse. No human being should be shaped like he was, bent backward at the midsection of his back. His eyes were wide open, as was his mouth. He was trying to form words, but couldn't, either from pain or paralysis, or both. He couldn't even manage to turn his head. Only when his eyes moved was Christine aware that he could see her.

"Russ. Shhh. It's not here right now."

He moaned again, his fingers coiling.

"Hel—" his words came out as an agonized whimper, "he—ee—lp me."

"Shhh, I will. Just wait," she said. "Just be quiet. I don't know where it's at. Give me a moment, I'll figure out which way leads out."

His hand found her ankle and squeezed. She kneeled down to comfort him, but with the sound of footsteps echoing behind her, she realized he wasn't grabbing her from pain, but intense fright.

It was coming back.

She wanted to scream. There was nowhere to hide. Nowhere to run. The section of tunnel behind the dead bodies likely led to a dead end, as the creature was entering the cave from the other side. She was trapped.

Think!

Her teeth clattered as though in Antarctic temperatures. She couldn't see it yet, but that would change any moment. The sounds seemed to be coming from above, rather than within.

First, she killed the light on her phone, once again entrapping her in darkness, with the exception of the illumination from her screen. The dark spurred the terror within Russ, causing him to whimper further.

"N—Neh—No."

"Shh, Russ, be quiet." She spoke so softly, she could barely hear her own voice. She could hear the thing starting to enter the cave. There was only one thing she could think to do: lay down where she was and play dead. At the very least it would buy her time. If worst came to worst, and it probably would, she would sprint for the exit and take her chances.

She tucked her phone into her pocket, pulled herself from Russ' grip, then leaned over briefly, whispering "lie still. Don't draw it's attention." She hurried over to her spot, then lay face-down.

Another orange light took form straight ahead. Christine closed one eye and squinted the other, discreetly watching the tunnel straight ahead while appearing dead.

The light was dancing. Fire. The thing had learned to invent fire. It lowered itself down the incline up ahead. No wonder she didn't see an exit that way; the tunnel angled up toward the surface.

She heard Russ moan again.

Oh, please, Russell, don't make any sound. It'll probably eat the pigs or goats first, and be too full to get to us. For Godsake! Be fucking quiet!" If it slumbered, they'd have a chance. All they needed to do was wait it out.

The beast growled, hunching over slightly as it stepped onto level ground. It gazed briefly at its kill, like a butcher arriving for the morning shift. Its tongue slipped out the decayed side of its face, licking the side of its teeth. A horrid stench radiated off its fur, bringing a bit of humidity into the tunnel. Christine suspected it had gotten water from the lake.

It carried a burning branch like a torch. The glow shone on its furry chest and neck, and the blood that spilled from its bullet wounds. It didn't appear overly concerned with those injuries, or the slash wound under its left armpit.

Did one of the hunters hit it with a knife? Then it came to her: *The bear.* She remembered the blood on its paws. It had gotten a slash in before being beaten to the ground. She wondered if that's why it wasn't taken for food. Perhaps they had battled, and in doing so, the bear hurt it, which in turn angered it. Instead of killing for hunger, Bigfoot had gone for simple, sweet revenge. Maybe the six-pointer at the lake did the same thing, hence its head was ripped away and discarded.

Or…maybe the beast just enjoyed killing.

It dragged something by its other arm. It was large, definitely a kill. The body rippled against the ground as it was pulled along. Christine's eye widened briefly upon the realization that it was dragging Beau Stevenson. His face was completely unrecognizable. The skin was intact, but it looked as though it had been peeled off the bone.

Her heart was practically drumming the ground under her chest right now. The humanoid sauntered by her, its huge foot stepping down within inches from her hand. Judging by its lack of concern, had it stepped on her and snapped bones, it wouldn't have paid it a single thought. Unless she screamed, in which case, she was additionally grateful it missed.

She almost did scream when Beau's dead hand touched hers. It felt cold and soft, yet rigid in the way dead things were. There was the mildest sense of relief when it was pulled away.

Christine heard Bigfoot walk a little further back, then crouch, like a camper setting up his fire. In fact, it appeared that that was exactly what it was doing. With the slowest of movements, Christine turned her head back. The beast was on its knees, putting dead wood together in a small pit which she hadn't noticed before. On the wall beside it were several broken branches, the edges of which were scraped bare until they were practically pointed spears.

What did it need those for in a cave? Defense? It could rip things apart with its bare hands. Hell, it beat a near-four-hundred pound bear until it was just a saggy piece of meat.

For several minutes the beast made its fire. Christine could feel the tunnel warming up. She wondered if this was a preference, or if the creature had a need for warmth. What was it doing? What was *it*?!

As the fire enlarged, Bigfoot reached down and grabbed one of the twigs it had collected. It lowered the tip to the flame, igniting it, then raised the now-burning tip to one of the wounds in its chest. The creature growled as it cauterized the wound.

With age brought experience. It knew how to seal injuries. Hell, as old as this thing was, living in a place like this, Christine wondered if its immune system was advanced. It had probably survived all kinds of diseases, and carried all of them. Judging by all the scabs in its body, and the decay in what used to be its left cheek, the beast was old and had survived many challenges thrown by nature.

It cauterized another wound. It was an animal of basic skill, like a caveman from the stone age. But it was still an animal. It had no sense of regret, compassion, disgust. The only emotion it probably did feel was hate, judging by the useless carnage she had seen.

The answer regarding the spear came immediately. It stood straight, its head slightly hunched under the dirt ceiling. It looked at the slaughterhouse that was its habitat, selected one of the dead pigs by its hind legs, then picked up one of the spears. Christine suppressed a whimper as it rammed the spear through the pig's rear, punching it up along its spine, until it came out through its neck. It had literally skewered the pig.

Christine wanted to look away, but was afraid that any movement would not go unnoticed, especially with the tunnel now illuminated by the flame. All she could do was watch as the Bigfoot propped the spit between two Y-shaped branches, which it drove into the ground on both sides of the fire. There, it let its meal cook. Meanwhile, it sauntered back into the cave, then picked something up.

There was a slight temptation to run while its back was turned. However, Christine couldn't bring herself to do it. She saw how the thing moved. She wouldn't get halfway to the entrance before she would be grabbed and impaled. She couldn't run. Yet, terror was slowly getting the better of her. She couldn't stay either! Watching the pig on the spit, she saw her own fate.

Adding to the nauseating feeling was the sight of the Bigfoot picking up a dead possum. It held the thing and ate it like a drumstick; an appetizer before the main course.

Now, bile was working its way into Christine's throat. Clearly, the thing didn't require meat to be cooked. So, what then? Did it discover the taste of cooked meat somewhere during its likely long life? How much could it eat? Was it going to cook everything in its lair? Clearly, it was a patient creature.

Several minutes passed.

Bigfoot tossed the remnants of the possum aside and returned to the pig. It turned the spit, waited a moment, then lifted it from the fire. There was a squelching sound of teeth mashing partially cooked flesh. It returned the pig to the flame, then stepped to the other side of the cave, munching as though it had just taken in a mouthful of potato chips.

Bits of flesh fell from the side of its mouth as it looked at the next corpse to skewer. It stood over the dead officers. Christine's heart rate doubled. She should have run. Perhaps she could take her chances right now. Just take off and pray that she would make it.

The thing knelt down. It grabbed Beau Stevenson's corpse by the ankle and pulled him toward the fire. The sound of fabric being torn echoed through the lair. Bigfoot ripped the clothing away, rendering Beau's limp corpse bare. It sniffed the clothing and belt, tasted it, figured it was not edible, and tossed it aside.

It grabbed another spear, lifted Beau up by the ankle, the other leg hanging free, then positioned the spear. This time, Christine shut her eyes, though that didn't block the gut-wrenching sound of the spear being forced up Beau's anus into his stomach.

Only with the sound of a whimper did she open her eyes again. The terror had not only gotten to her, but to Russ as well. The poor young officer broke, having watched Beau get skewered like a roast. Bigfoot tossed its prize next to the flame, then whipped around toward the paralyzed officer. It stared, seemingly fascinated with the physical condition of its prey.

Christine's world was spinning. This could not be happening. She couldn't bear to watch or listen to this. Yet, there was no choice. She prayed, though she didn't know who to. She settled on God and begged that Russ would die of fright. Or something. ANYTHING! As long as it was instantaneous and right now. Or even just fall unconscious. At least that would spare him any further abuse.

But no such wish was granted. Russ was moaning loudly. Between those moans were high-pitched squeals. He was trying to scream, but the action of doing so triggered intense spasms in his spine. His nerves were lighting up along his body like high-voltage wires.

Bigfoot approached, then stood over him. It growled, watching the paralyzed officer trying to work his arms. It seemed…amused. The worst sounding squeal…so far…came when it picked up Russ by the heel. It tossed him by the fire then knelt down.

No. Don't…Christine continued begging for Russ to die or pass out right there. Now, it wasn't just for his sake, but for hers.

The next sound was that of clothes being torn from the body. The beast started with his shirt and undershirt, shredding them into ribbons and tossing them away. Then it ripped at his pants, boxers, boots, and socks, until Russ was lying on the ground naked. Bigfoot inspected the clothing again, tossed it to the side, then turned around to reach for another branch-spear.

"N-n-NO!" Russ screamed.

Christine couldn't help herself. She cupped a hand to her mouth and pressed tight. It took everything to keep from screaming. Only because Bigfoot's back was turned, he did not notice her. That, and the fact that he was focused on the next course of action.

This time, it was a full scream that escaped Russ' lungs as he was lifted by his right ankle. Bigfoot spun him back, then pressed the spear into his anus. That scream intensified, and no nerve pain could stop the writhing motion that resulted from the sensation of a ten-foot branch slowly stabbing through his bowels. Blood spilled from his mouth as it entered his intestines and stomach region, and the scream turned into a gurgle as the spear cut through one of his lungs. As the tip emerged from the side of his neck, his body was still spasming. After several seconds, Russ Linn was finally limp, save for a few twitches resulting from muscular reflex

Instead, it was Christine who passed out.

CHAPTER 17

The forest was becoming a blur. It was not an effect of the night or the whistling breeze that kicked up every few minutes. Nor was it a result of fatigue. Robert Windle was starting to sense that there was something wrong with him as he and Shane Alter trekked through the woods.

At first, he simply chalked it up as a consequence of the shock of seeing Jake Cobb decapitated in front of him, followed by that of nearly getting killed himself. In addition to that, he watched three officers get brutally slaughtered, and his fiancé...*ex*-fiancé, get taken into the woods.

And here he was now, off to her rescue with the man who, in his mind, stole her away from him.

Hot air escaped his nostrils, especially whenever he looked at the cop. The dumb prick caused all of this. *He* was the one who made the hunters wait, intently to keep Robert away from Christine.

Feeling a little jealous, huh?

Robert shook his head. Clearly, the previous events had agitated him, but now he was just feeling inexplicably angry. His temples felt like they were squeezing his brain. His shoulder felt terrible where the thing had clawed him. It didn't hurt this much before. Perhaps his brain didn't register it fully at the time due to the chaos. He would have settled for that explanation were it not for the pain everywhere else in his body. Even his knuckles felt as though they were on the verge of bursting through his skin.

Something wasn't right. Though he was worried, he simply was feeling angry. There was an urge to hit Shane. Anyone really. Any*thing*. He just wanted to lash out.

His stomach churned. Robert swallowed, winced, then kept walking. The throbbing intensified. He glanced down at the pistol he held, which shook in his hand. Not trusting himself with it at the moment, he tucked it in his waist. His mind briefly contemplated turning back. Maybe Shane was right about waiting for backup.

NO! I'm not going to let this prick be the one to save her.

Robert convinced himself that he was fine, despite the fact that he was gradually slowing down.

Flashlights swayed back and forth, finding traces of blood, and small grooves in the leave blanket that covered the earth. Something had been dragged through here. The worst part was that they suspected what, or rather *who* it was. They had decided to briefly check the lakeside, where Shane discovered that Beau Stevenson's body had disappeared. The rock that crushed his skull was still there, caked with blood.

Shane wasn't sure if the blood in the trail was Bigfoot's or the officer's. It didn't matter in the end, as long as it led them to wherever the creature was hiding.

As they walked, he could hear Robert clearing his throat, the way a man did when he was trying to fight down nausea. He glanced back at the hunter.

"You alright?"

"Fine!" Robert's words came like a bullet. Oddly enough, it seemed as though it was intended to be as vicious. Shane noticed he wasn't holding the pistol. Odd choice, considering the creature out there could arrive at any given moment. Should it appear, the split-second to draw the weapon could mean the difference between life and death. Still, Shane didn't question it. He could see in Robert's eyes that the guy was on edge. Nerves probably. Who could blame him?

Shane led then for another hundred yards. Low branches reached down at them like bony claws from undead corpses. Aside from the wind, there was hardly a sound to be heard. He felt as though he was walking through a graveyard. The chill of the night air didn't help. He regretted not keeping his jacket. Yeah, it was full of ants, but he could've shaken them out and kept it.

Dry leaves crumbled under his boots as loud as snapping twigs. He paused briefly. He would never look at autumn the same way again. It was probably his favorite season, aside from late spring. Summer was nice, but often got too hot for his tastes. He tried to focus on good memories from all of these seasons, but all these heavenly thoughts did was remind him of the hell he was in currently.

There was nothing but night air between the trees. Every square foot of open space played mind games with him. It felt as though something would jump out at them at any time. And when something did, it was doubly worse.

Shane shrieked when the squirrel darted in front of him. Being a foot long didn't matter. First, there was nothing there, then suddenly he saw movement. He pointed his pistol, but managed to keep from squeezing the trigger. Had he practiced poor trigger discipline, he would have discharged several shots like a rookie. The fact that his finger pressed on the trigger guard confirmed this fact.

"God!" he hissed. He sucked in a breath through clenched teeth. Was the whole forest trying to mess with his mind? It certainly felt like it.

Next was the sound of vomiting.

Shane turned around and saw Robert hunched over, letting it loose behind a tree. He coughed and heaved again, then leaned against a nearby tree. This didn't look like a man suffering from anxiety only. He looked...ill.

"You sure you're alright, Robert?" Shane asked. "Seriously? You don't seem well."

Robert straightened his stance, though not yet turning to face the officer.

"You *expect* me to be doing well?" he said.

"You know what I mean," Shane replied. He approached the hunter and shone his light onto his injured shoulder. There was a lot of blood there. Robert saw the alarm in his expression.

"It's not all mine," he said. "You guys hit the bastard pretty hard. Too bad it didn't seem to accomplish much."

Shane didn't respond to that. Instead, he leaned closer. "Turn your head toward me, please."

Robert scoffed. "Why? Want a kiss?"

"Dude, shut the fuck up and just do what I ask."

Robert sighed, then held still. "You a doctor now?" Shane didn't answer. Instead, the alarmed facial expression resurfaced.

"Dude, your eyes are bloodshot," he said. He placed a hand to Robert's brow. "Shit. You're burning up."

"Dude I'm fine," Robert said. "We just got attacked by a freaking sasquatch. My body temp might be up a tad."

"This isn't a tad. You're on fire, man," Shane said. "We need to get you to a hospital."

"Shane, shut the fu—" Robert doubled over as a new wave of pain rippled through him. His shoulder felt like it was going to explode. His joints, while bent, felt like they were being stretched. His skull felt as though it was in a decompression generator. He turned away and dry-heaved.

"Case and point," Shane said.

"I just need a breather," Robert said. He lowered himself to the ground, then sat against the base of a tree. At this point, Shane couldn't take his eyes off the wound. After holstering his Glock, he knelt beside the hunter and reached for the ribbons of clothing near his shoulder. Robert shot him a glare. "What are you doing?"

"JUST...Let me check."

Shane pulled at the gap in the clothing, causing Robert to shake in pain. The officer ignored the cursing that followed as he inspected the injury. There was blood all around the lacerations. Robert would certainly need stitches, but that wasn't what concerned Shane the most. The skin was clearly discolored. Veins had turned purple all over his chest and shoulder. The shoulder itself looked enlarged, but not from swelling. The musculature looked rather…enhanced, though grotesque at the same time.

Shane then noticed the bulging in areas of skin as well as the discoloration of veins in Robert's neck. There was no question; the Bigfoot was carrying disease of some kind. Probably in its nails, hence the worst of the infection was around the actual injury.

"Yeah, man, we've gotta get you some treatment."

"No!" Robert said. "Not until we find her."

"You won't do her much good like this," Shane replied.

"Yeah? Like *you* did?"

"I—" Shane stopped, realizing he was about to chase a red herring.

"She wouldn't be in this predicament if she stuck with me."

"She's a cop, Robert. Of course, she went out there with me," Shane replied.

"Sure. *That's* the reason," Robert groaned.

"Dude, I've never met you before today. I don't know the history between you and her, but for chrissake, this is not the time." Shane glanced around, hoping their conversation wasn't drawing the attention of the beast. He remembered how Beau thought he saw it, which Shane now believed. And yet, it managed to keep out of sight, despite its size and weight. It had probably been tracking them for as long as they were out there, and for all he knew, it could be tracking them now. And he would never know it, until it emerged from hiding, claws outstretched.

He wanted to keep searching for Christine, but he couldn't keep Robert out here in this condition. Splitting up would be suicide. He was stuck with an impossible decision.

The sensation of being shoved backward by Robert interrupted his thoughts. He caught his balance, tempted momentarily to retaliate but resisted, partially out of fear of attracting the beast, and partially because he was surprised from the strength Robert demonstrated.

"Dude!" he whispered harshly. "I'm trying to help you!"

"Bullshit. This is about Christine," Robert said, not bothering to lower his voice.

"Yes, it's about Christine. And you're in no condition to keep going after her. You can barely keep yourself up."

"Yeah-yeah, knight in shining armor," Robert muttered. Shane didn't know what to say. He felt like he was talking to someone who had lost his mind. Perhaps that was the case. God only knew how high a temperature Robert's fever had climbed to. "You just don't want ME to be the one to find her. Probably because you know I'm better for her than you are."

"What the—" Shane closed his eyes. *This can't be happening.* Was this night destined to get worse with each passing minute? Not only was he in the woods at night with a murderous beast somewhere beyond sight, with his girlfriend missing, possibly dead, but he was stuck alongside this guy, who was an egotistical moron to begin with, now suffering from some kind of delusion.

It didn't help knowing that Robert was armed.

Robert coughed some more, wiped his sleeve over his brow, then took a deep breath.

"I'm good," he said. He sounded as though he was trying to convince himself, rather than Shane. He held his hands out, almost seeming repentant of his recent words and actions. "I'm good. I'm fine. Let's just get through this." Without waiting for a reply, he continued walking northwest.

Shane watched him, particularly his hands, hoping they wouldn't go for the pistol. This whole situation was unprecedented, and the fact that Robert's condition had deteriorated in such a short amount of time concerned him greatly. At this stage, he wouldn't be surprised if the guy had another angry outburst. If so, would he go for the pistol and try to shoot Shane out of spite? Yet, attempting to disarm him would likely spark such an action. Shane felt like he had no good options except to stay behind Robert and watch him closely.

"Fuck me."

He slowly drew his weapon and kept it pointed down as he continued on. Only now, it wasn't only what he couldn't see that concerned him.

CHAPTER 18

Christine awoke with a slight shutter. Immediately, she wanted to cry when she still felt the dirt under her face. It wasn't a nightmare. She was still here in the creature's lair. The sound of chewing and ripping nearly got the better of her weakened senses.

She wasn't sure how long she was out, but it was long enough for a new stench to fill the tunnel. The smell of searing flesh would forever be ingrained in her memory, as would the sight of the beast sitting by its flame. It held onto one of the spears like corn-on-the-cob. The sight of the mangled, blackened corpse skewered at its center nearly made her pass out again. The legs were still intact, as was most of the pelvis. The head had come off clean, as did the right arm. The torso had been stripped to the bone. The jagged spine confirmed it was what remained of Russ Linn.

She couldn't see Beau, which was probably for the best. Behind her fear was a feeling of contempt. Why did she have to wake up?

Just stay asleep so I don't have to be impaled.

If she was able to get out of here, she would never be able to look at meat the same way ever again. It'd be a week before she'd be able to even eat anything at all at this point. She was never a fan of the vegan, or even the vegetarian lifestyle, but this might push her over.

The creature paid no mind to its other kills as its jaws tore another strip of flesh from the legs. It munched, while staring at the wall across from it. Then it belched.

The resulting stench was even worse than the charred meat.

A tear streamed from Christine's eye. Once again, her mind went through all the usual plans of actions, only to settle on nothing. Even now, she was still too terrified to run. She needed a good head start if she was going to have any kind of chance. Simply sprinting would not cut it.

Just go to sleep. PLEASE.

Her heart jumped as the creature stood up. It tossed the skeletal remains to the back of the tunnel, then stretched its arms. Christine wondered if her wish would come true. Was it going to rest? Was this her chance?

The beast waited, then burped again. It moved a few things with its feet which Christine couldn't see, then started glancing about. Her mind got fixed on the possibility that the thing was making room to lay down and snooze. Instead, it turned around and grabbed another spear.

No, please...

It gazed at its many kills, clearly still hungry. It was acting on appetite: determining which victim would taste the best.

Her heart stopped as its eyes turned in her direction. Next came the crunching of dirt under its feet. It was approaching. She could feel her blood racing, causing tiny tremors throughout her body. Despite this, she remained motionless.

The beast stopped, tilted its head, then reached down. It grabbed Walter by the ankle and proceeded to pull him toward the fire. Christine felt a sense of relief, which was accompanied with guilt. Of course, Walter was already dead, so she really had nothing to be guilty about.

Focus on your own survival.

There was no telling how much more it would consume. One thing was certain, however: it enjoyed the taste of human flesh, which meant she was high on its list. The already slim chances of survival had dropped even further. She couldn't risk waiting for a slumber that may not even come. She had to escape NOW.

The sound of clothes ripping made it hard to focus. She closed her eyes and tried to think of something. She had no weapons, other than a small pocketknife. Common sense told her that she'd never get close enough to even prick the skin. There was nothing in this cave she could throw at it that would do any good.

She shuddered as Bigfoot shrieked. She opened her eyes, seeing it backing off from the flame. It dropped Walter and checked its leg briefly, then snatched him back up and returned to work.

It almost seemed like a tease. Fire—too bad she didn't have the strength to shove the thing into its own flame. Hell, the only fire she had was from...

Her cigarette lighter.

Christine's mind went to work figuring out a plan. She had access to fire right there in her pocket. Though, it was a tiny flame, which would do almost nothing to something as large as the creature. She could try and make the flame bigger, but unless Bigfoot was willing to hold still, there was no way she would hurt him long enough to buy time to escape. But the idea had merit. She was so close, yet so far. If only she had something to enhance the flame instantaneously. A butane cannister. Gas. Anything.

Now, along with being fearful, she was getting angry. This wasn't fair! The prospect of a weapon, but insufficient tools to utilize it was torture in itself. She would be better off trying to run. After all, she had nothing to fight with except a cigarette lighter, a pocketknife, and bullets without a gun to shoot them.

Bullets. Gunpowder. Which burns like a motherfucker!

Her hand slowly felt for her magazine. It was full, containing seventeen bullets. All she needed to do was pry the bullet from its casing. If only she had pliers to do it.

The answer was simple: simply use the pocketknife. It was a folding knife with a serrated edge. She just needed to close the knife to press the bullet tightly between the blade and handle, twist it, and free the gunpowder from the casing. It was an unconventional method, but nothing that couldn't be pulled off.

A few bullets would provide enough powder to do the trick. She just needed enough to distract the brute long enough for her to get a running start. Did the creature understand how to put out fires? Probably, since it clearly knew how to start them. Then again, gunpower burns were different from regular fire.

It was a crazy idea, but it was better than any other option she had.

The creature's left shoulder was pointed toward her, its head tilted down to allow its eyes to focus on its task. Like the previous human victims, it studied the clothing with interest, then tossed them aside.

Christine took the chance. Her left hand inched slowly toward her magazine pouch. Her fingers trembled, not out of fear, but because of restraint. It took all of her willpower to not snatch the item and move quickly, which would only result in her demise.

Her fingertips reached the pouch. It was covered by a strap which was secured by a snap. Popping it open was not difficult in itself, but in a dense cave like this, the tiniest sound could reverberate. Christine hesitated, her eyes fixed on the beast. It completed tearing away the clothing, then glanced about for its stick, which it had set down during the process.

It turned about, those eyes settling on Christine.

Sweat poured down her brow. Blood rushed like river rapids. It saw her. Her arm was in a different place. It had to have noticed. It was going to kill her now. She had failed…

The beast stepped forward.

No choice now. Get up and run…

It leaned forward and found the spear where it had inadvertently placed it when collecting its next meal. Subsequently, it turned around and returned to the fire.

She wasted no time relishing in her relief. She unclipped the strap as gently as she could, then pulled the magazine to her chest. Next, she went for her pocketknife. Her eyes traded off between the task and the beast, who was now in the process of spearing Walter.

Her body shook with the dry-heave that escaped. Luckily, she was able to keep it quiet. She partially unfolded the pocketknife, then, as gently as possible, slipped the first bullet out of the magazine. She pinched the nine-millimeter round by the casing, then squeezed the knife down on the bullet. The serrated edge lodged it perfectly. Next, she twisted the knife like a wrench. It took a little effort, but thankfully the bullet didn't resist too badly. She lifted it away from the casing, revealing the gunpowder inside.

A quiet sigh of relief, which was then followed by the realization that she didn't have anything to store the powder in. There was no way she could handle numerous open casings without dropping and spilling much of her powder supply. She needed one storage unit. A dice cup. A thermos. Anything. It didn't have to be huge.

The stress brought forth her intense craving for a cigarette. *Oh God. Not that.* It was just another distraction in an impossible situation. She slipped the next bullet out while Bigfoot was still facing away, then got to work on removing the bullet. This one came out a little faster. She was getting the hang of it.

That stupid craving wouldn't go away. It was like something was pulling at her throat from the inside. Perhaps she could satisfy the oral fixation by putting one of the cigs between her teeth. She was growing more confident in moving slightly faster. Confident or eager, she wasn't sure.

Bigfoot placed the impaled Walter over the fire, then took a seat against the wall. It then proceeded to pick its teeth with a twig.

Christine had the cigarette case in hand. Luckily, she was well covered in shadow, so the white paper case didn't stand out too much. Still, she didn't want to risk drawing attention to herself, and she wasn't going to smoke the thing anyway, so she broke off the butt and stuffed it between her teeth.

She found herself staring into the pack. Right there, it dawned on her: she did have a container after all. She gently reached behind her back and dumped the cigarette, then set the empty pack down by her stomach. The creature did not notice. It turned the spit, causing the dead man's limbs to sway like tree branches.

It was impossible to ignore the smell of flesh being charred. The fact that it was a human being made it a hundred times worse. Then there was the reality that it was Walter…

She forced it out of her mind. *Don't look.*

She didn't. She emptied the two casings into the cigarette pack, then went to work on the next bullet. Just a few more would do the trick.

I'll sear some meat of my own.

She had her BIC lighter out. As she quietly pried the next bullet from its casing, another concern came to mind: the size and sustainability of the flame. Yeah, it would only take a touch of the flame to ignite the powder, but in a situation like this, would she even be able to hold down the button long enough? Those flames were easy to lose.

Christine wasted no time debating with herself mentally; she would have to remove the flame shield and twist the nozzle to enlarge the flame and increase the butane release.

But that would have to wait for last. For now, she had other work to do.

CHAPTER 19

Shane couldn't take his eyes off of Robert as he followed him through the woods. The man was hunched over now. He hadn't seen his face in the last half-hour or so, nor was any word spoken between them. However, Shane understood the body language. Something was wrong, and it was obvious it had something to do with the infection.

Shane could not get the image of that bloody wound from his mind. The veins, the discoloration, the odd misshapen shoulder. Something was happening to Robert, and whatever it was, it was happening fast. His mind raced to figure out a solution, while leaping over the hurdles of questions in its way. Did the Bigfoot really carry such a strong, fast acting infection? If so, would that mean it carried the infection in its fur? The thought was too terrible to contemplate. Was he infected too and just didn't know it? What if this creature was carrying something as terrible as the Black Plague?

It couldn't be, though. If such a thing was that easily transmitted, there'd be traces of it all over the forest. They'd be seeing sick animals everywhere. As far as Shane knew, he hadn't seen anything. Just animals half-devoured or crushed to death, like the horses, deer, and the bear.

He slowed as he recalled finding the bear's corpse. The blood on the paw that didn't appear to be its own...and the possum that looked like it was sick. He had seen the creature scurry from the bear's arm. Was it licking the blood? What was happening to it?

The blood...

"It's not all mine." Robert had said. It was all coming together. Bigfoot's blood splattered onto Robert and had gotten into his wound. The blood was infectious.

The hunter dropped to his knees.

Shane sprinted toward him. "Hey, man. You alright?"

"Fine!"

He didn't sound fine. He barely sounded like Robert. He almost sounded like a ferocious beast of the wild. Still, Shane approached.

"Let me take another look..." He touched his hand to Robert's shoulder, who spun around to face him. His eyes were enlarged, bloodshot, and bulging from their sockets. His chest and shoulders were distended, as were his arms. His jaw was crooked, the teeth spaced out slightly. His arms were somewhat elongated, the fingers like werewolf claws.

The man was mutating in front of him.

Robert's face was a mixture of rage and panic.

"I—I don't know what's happening to me!" Even as he whimpered, he sounded more animal than human. When he stood up, Shane realized he was almost six inches taller than before. His belt was straining against its buckle. His boots were stretching. His shirt was tearing at the collar and wrists.

Shane felt as though he was watching something out of a *Marvel* film. Except, this was nothing so comical. This was terrifying, wet with saliva and blood, and filled with pain.

Those bulging eyes were fixed on the officer, who was stumbling backward. He raised his gun a few degrees but still kept it low. He still couldn't bring himself to shoot a human being. Then again, it was hard to think of Robert Windle that way anymore.

The terror turned to sorrow.

"YOU! You got her into this! You did this to *me!*"

"Robert!" Shane held a hand out as a gesture of peace. "Please. You need a doctor."

Robert writhed in pain. Clothing ripped. The Glock fell from his waist. In any other circumstance, Shane would have been grateful for that, but now, Robert's possession of a firearm was not his concern.

His jaw hyperextended, his back arched with a loud *crack,* and he let out a high-pitched agonized squeal into the air. For a moment, he was crying. Then he was snarling, as though all remnants of his humanity were being stripped away as he transformed into an animal.

Robert covered his face with his hands, whose veins were protruding, some even bursting. He yelped again, then stood still. He lowered his hands, revealing a face with peeled back lips, a shrunken nose, and two eyes that looked as though they would pop like cherries any moment.

"You got her killed!"

Words. He still was human to an extent—in terms of species.

He took a step forward, his fingers hooked like bird talons. He was hunched over slightly, slowly coiling his arms like a praying mantis. Another step.

"Robert…" Shane warned, his finger twitching against the trigger. "Please. Don't."

"Don't?!" His voice was so deep, it was almost what Shane imagined a grizzly would sound like if it spoke. "Don't?! DON'T?!"

Was he taunting him, or just repeating the word like he just discovered language?

"DON'T?!"

Shane backed up. "Jesus."

"JESUS?! DON'T?!"

Shane felt no other choice than to raise his pistol. But Robert's sprint was faster. Shane went to sidestep, narrowly avoiding getting impaled by those fingers, but failing to evade the backhand that followed. He hit the ground and skidded for several feet. His fingers closed on nothing. The Glock was gone. All he had was the flashlight. He beamed it at Robert, who covered his face. His eyelids hadn't mutated yet to compensate for the bulging eyes.

"JESUS! DON'T!"

It was just a momentary delay. Shane sucked in a breath as the Robert-thing advanced.

CHAPTER 20

The smell of smoke and meat assaulted Christine's nostrils, spurring the urge to move fast. Her hands shook violently with each twist of the knife. It was a constant fight against her own instincts. She glanced at the Bigfoot only to gauge whether she was in its line of sight. Twice, she had to play dead when it turned around. In doing so, she kept an arm over the bullet casings and cigarette pack to prevent suspicion.

She had a perfect opportunity now, as the beast wandered to the back of the cave out of sight. After removing the bullet, she poured the powder into the cigarette case. She had emptied eight bullets now. It would have to be enough. Now, she needed to fix the issue of the lighter.

First, she closed her eyes and took a deep breath, forcing herself to maintain control over her nerves. She exhaled slowly, feeling some of the tension release. Time to work.

First thing's first: she had to remove the flame shield. She opened the knife fully then pressed the blade under the paper-thin notch under the shield. The blade scraped over it the first few times. She pressed the edge down, as though attempting to cut through the plastic itself, then raked the blade against the shield. This time, it caught the edge of the shield. It took a little effort, but she was able to pry it off successfully, revealing the nozzle.

Damn. I need tweezers to twist this thing to the right.

"Fuck," she whispered. Eyeing her serrated knife-blade, she angled it against the nozzle. She scraped it to the right as though trying to generate a spark from the friction, which was barely enough to turn the nozzle. Each time only turned it a tiny bit, which forced her to do it repeatedly.

"Come on. Come on…"

She heard footsteps. Her eyes looked to the flame. Bigfoot was returning. It turned the spit, then prepared to sit down by the fire. Its eyes turned toward Christine, who lay perfectly still.

It looked away briefly. Christine started to resume her task, only to stop when the beast turned toward her again. There was suspicion in those eyes, which reflected the orange-yellow glow of the fire.

It wasn't looking away this time.

Christine was aware that she had shifted her position during her prep. It was clear that the beast had taken notice. Its head tilted slightly, the eyes looking at something slightly to the right of her. Very slowly, Christine turned her head slightly.

One of the casings had rolled into the center of the cave. It reflected the glow of the fire like a tiny mirror, resembling a star in the middle of the dark tunnel. Bigfoot stoop up suddenly. The movement was so fast and so vicious, there was no withholding the reactionary shake. Its eyes went back to Christine.

It knew the truth now.

She got up on her knees and pressed the knife against the nozzle again.

"Come on!" she said loudly. Bigfoot roared and advanced. His footsteps echoed through the tunnel. Christine raked the knife again and again, until the nozzle could go no further. Butane escaped freely.

The beast was almost on top of her. With the next step, it was within reach.

Christine snatched up the pack full of gunpowder then clicked the flint wheel. A two-inch flame escaped, burning nonstop. Bigfoot stopped, saw that the tiny flame was no threat, then reached for her.

"You forgot your seasoning."

She threw the powder at the beast, spreading it all over its chest. It was do or die. She leapt at him with the flame, touching it to the powder that settled on its fur.

An earsplitting roar tore through the cave as Bigfoot's chest went ablaze. Clawing at the flame as though it was a swarm of ants crawling over him, the beast staggered backward, right into his own flame behind him. Another huge bellow shook the earth. Now, its right leg was ablaze.

Christine's plan had worked, much to her own surprise. Even more surprising, she actually had to make herself run for it. She had thought it would've been instantaneous, but the sight of the burning beast was so horrific, yet fascinating, it was hard to look away. But she did, and within seconds, she had sprinted to the mouth of the cave. It angled upward near the end, forcing her to climb on all fours to reach the mouth.

Behind her, the beast was throwing itself against the walls, struggling to extinguish the fire.

Christine pulled herself out, embracing the pure clean air. As much as she hated wandering through Oak Grove Forest on this night, compared to that cave, it was practically paradise.

The beast was running toward the cave. She looked down through the entrance, seeing the glow of its smoldering body. It was still putting out the fire WHILE trying to catch her.

It roared again as she ran into the woods. Clawing at the tunnel's edge, it pulled itself up after her. Fire danced over its right shoulder, while smoke twirled from its leg. The beast launched itself onto the earth's surface, only to fall to the ground and roll. Its agonized movements assisted in defeating the fire, leaving a raw, hairless stretch of flesh that ran from its center chest to its upper shoulder.

It roared again, the voice carrying through the forest like thunder.

CHAPTER 21

Only when he heard the echo, did Robert halt his murderous advance on Shane. He had his arm raised, ready to grab the officer and rip the entrails out from his body. Instead, he stopped and looked northwest into the forest. Shane simply watched, completely at Robert's mercy. Should the man-thing he had become proceed with the slaughter, there would be no escape.

However, it seemed Robert's interest in him had vanished in an instant. Instead, it almost seemed as though a memory had been triggered. That roar was the beast he was initially after…the beast that had taken his love. It was somewhere beyond those trees.

In the blink of an eye, Robert had run off into the forest. Shane felt frozen, only managing to turn his head slightly just in time to catch a glimpse of Robert disappearing into the darkness.

Somewhere in that darkness was the Bigfoot…and possibly Christine. He couldn't give up on her yet. If he turned back and she was still alive, the misery would be worse than any horror they endured this night.

He stood up, located the two firearms, then ran after Robert.
****

Christine could hear it running behind her. She had come so close, she HAD to keep going.

"HELP!" she screamed, certain there was nobody in this forest able to help her. The adrenaline pushed her along, but as with all living things, fatigue was setting in. She had lost tons of energy from the tension alone, and she was still somewhat groggy from passing out.

She didn't dare look back—just hearing the thumps of its running feet was enough. And those thumps were gradually getting louder. The only sound matching those steps was that of her frantic breathing.

There was another sound; more running footsteps, only this time they were ahead of her.

She found her smartphone and triggered the flashlight setting, sending a white stream into the forest around her. She raised it over her head like a beacon, signaling to anyone out here where she was. There was no consideration that she was leading the beast to any other people in these woods, as in the moment, she couldn't think that far ahead.

Pointing the light ahead, she saw the silhouette of someone running at her. She quickly recognized the torn camouflage jacket that was Robert's. For the first time in a year, she could not have been happier to see him.

"Over here!" she screamed.

Only when Robert came within twenty feet did she realize he was over half-a-foot taller. His lips were peeled back like an onion, revealing teeth that had stretched a full centimeter. Fluid seeped from his ballooned eyes. His skin was discolored into shades of yellow and red. His shoulders were hunched, his limbs stretched, fingers like spears.

Christine gasped, then stumbled backward, her phone falling from her grip. The flashlight beamed straight upward, lighting the space between her and Robert. She could not manage a scream. It was as though her vocals were paralyzed. She stumbled backward from the thing that was her ex-fiancé.

Robert stepped toward her and held out a hand, palm up. He tried to say something, but it just came out as a growly moan with several syllables. Then, it turned into a full sneer. He straightened his stance and glared past her.

Christine could feel the weight of Bigfoot's mass pounding the earth just a few meters behind her. She took off in a sprint, zigzagging past Robert, who held his ground against the beast.

Bigfoot slowed to a stop, his interest in the human temporarily halted while he faced this new challenger. It was a beast of his making, though he lacked that understanding. To Bigfoot, Robert was just a swollen version of his previous self. For a beast that had survived for countless generations, having devoured creatures of all shapes and sizes, vertebrates and invertebrates, Robert's horrid appearance meant nothing. He would taste just as delicious over the fire as any forest critter or human.

The Robert-thing held his ground, his mind conflicted between the hyper-aggression he experienced and the natural urge to flee. The human part of his brain knew he had no chance against the Bigfoot. However, there was a new side to him. An animalistic side. Like a virus, it killed all that was human, leaving a mutated, misshapen organ that was his brain. There was no true fear, only hunger, and an intense urge to kill.

He was the first to charge.

The determination and ambitiousness of the smaller creature was almost amusing to Bigfoot, who only budged a few small steps from Robert's futile attempts to wrestle it to the ground.

Christine ran as fast as she could, blinded by darkness, her mind almost lost to the terror around her. It sounded like a dogfight was taking place behind her. Enraged roaring filled the canopy, the vibrations shaking the leaves from their branches.

She only made a hundred feet or so before tripping over a dead branch. Tumbling head over heels, she settled on the ground face-up. She was lost. She didn't know which direction she was going. She was alone, doomed to be claimed by whoever won the brawl taking place behind her.

"Christine!"

Her mind registered the voice as soon as she saw the glow of the flashlight. She sat up and looked to her left. A flashlight, drawing closer and closer. She jumped to her feet and waved her arms.

"Over here!"

Shane stopped briefly, panned to his left just a few feet, then spotted her. Both ran and closed the distance, embracing each other in their arms. They exchanged kisses, full of relief neither never thought they'd experience. Both had been certain the other was dead by now, and that they'd never see each other again.

The moment of levity was brief, as the sound of roaring beasts reminded them of their predicament.

Bigfoot absorbed another slash to his abdomen, his opponent failing to break his thick skin. Enough was enough. Bigfoot lunged, snatching the mutated human by both shoulders and lifting him high. Like a wrestler, he slammed the mutation to the earth, resulting in a thunderous *crash*.

Before dealing the killing blow, a waving white light in the distance caught Bigfoot's attention. Taking his eyes off the human-thing pinned beneath his knee, he watched the dancing light. Within its glow was the female that deceived him and set him on fire. Standing beside her was the male whom it had left to die in the pit.

Two cunning humans who had harmed and outwitted it. An anger filled the Bigfoot, who roared his fury at the two as they retreated southeast.

Robert snarled, his ribs cracking under his enemy's weight. His nose took in the smell of burnt flesh along Bigfoot's chest and shoulder. Without hesitation, he raked his claws along the injury. Nerves flared, causing Bigfoot to rise off of his enemy. Robert was quickly on his feet. He understood that brute force was not the answer, and that he had to rely on agility. He pressed the attack, leaping several feet high and latching onto the beast. Claws and teeth found their way to the sensitive flesh, causing the Bigfoot to shriek.

Robert held on like a demented cat, even hissing while assaulting the damaged flesh. The skin was weaker here, splitting easily under his teeth. Fingers plunged into the skin, then pried into the muscular tissue underneath.

Blood ran down the Bigfoot's chest. No longer was it amused by the much smaller opponent. Now, its mind was warped with pain and agitation. It grabbed at the human-thing, closing its fingers around the right arm, prying the claws out of its flesh. Strands of tissue and blood stretched as the fingers emerged from the breaches they created. Bigfoot pushed with his other hand, the palm against Robert's torso. Slowly, he was separated from the brute, taking a mouthful of flesh with him.

He writhed in the Bigfoot's grip, eager to attack again. Even with his superior strength, Bigfoot was struggling to maintain his grip. Turning his whole body around, he swung Robert like a baseball bat, launching him several meters into the woods. Robert's squeal was muffled by the *crash* resulting from his impact with a large tree. The shockwave shook his body, preceding a second one which resulted from him hitting the ground afterwards.

Robert was facedown. He could tell something was broken. Nerves were shooting down both legs and there was a crunching pain in his right abdomen. Had he still possessed the critical thinking he had as a human, he would have considered the possibility of a cracked spinal column. However, he was an animal now, and the only critical thought he had left was the different methods he could kill.

He pushed himself to his feet, gasping from sudden bursts of pain that hit like lightning strikes. Pain—it was a reminder he was still alive, and nothing other than death would serve as an obstacle to victory.

He rushed another attack, but failed to jump, as his legs could not muster the strength. He aimed high to cut into the Bigfoot's sensitive burn injuries, only for his wrist to be snatched in a gorilla-like grip. Robert writhed in pain as Bigfoot sadistically twisted his arm. The beast twisted until the human-thing was on his knees and hunched over.

Even then, Bigfoot kept twisting, locking Robert's arm out. Finally, he pulled up. There was a dull *pop*, followed by a series of cracks. Robert cried out as his elbow bent backward. And still, Bigfoot kept pulling. Tendons and flesh stretched then tore free. Bigfoot held the forearm high like a trophy, while stomping its heel into Robert's ribcage to roll him onto his back. It stomped again, planting its foot on the injured opponent's chest to make sure he could watch as Bigfoot tasted the blood from the stump. Robert tried to push the foot off with his remaining hand, but his strength was quickly fading. Blood rapidly pumped from his elbow, literally draining him of energy, while Bigfoot drove the breath from his lungs.

Taunting his fallen enemy further, Bigfoot gnawed at the flesh on the arm. *This is what the future has in store for you.* After finishing, the beast tossed the boned limb into the woods, then lifted Robert off the ground with its hands. It carried him to the nearest tree, then, holding him by the heels, banged him against it like a bean bag. Bark covered in blood exploded off the trunk, the underlayers quickly becoming caked with blood and brains. Bigfoot smashed him repeatedly, rupturing the skull until it was a loose amoeba hanging between the shoulders.

Bigfoot threw the twitching body to the ground and proceeded to beat it with its fists. It pounded until every bone was broken, leaving the corpse a deflated, bloody thing.

It stood tall and triumphant.

There was no time to waste. There were two other humans left. The female would die slowly and painfully. Bigfoot could already envision her fate. It would break off all four limbs, cauterize them to make sure she didn't bleed out, then roast her torso while she was still breathing.

First, he had to catch her.

CHAPTER 22

"Alright. I think this is the road here," Deputy Page stated over the radio. Trooper Elijah Letson groaned. This would be the fourth wrong turn they'd made in the past twenty minutes. The Oak Grove Police dispatcher had been blowing up their airwaves, insinuating that they had lost all contact with the officers on scene.

"You guys ought to patrol up here a little more often," he replied to the deputies. "We would've gotten more useful information from a UPS driver."

"Bite me, Trooper," Deputy Rickenburg replied.

"You'd like that, wouldn't you," Elijah retorted.

"Or maybe you would," Trooper Alex McDermott said.

"What I'd like is to get this job finished up. How in the hell do these County patrollers not know their way around here?"

"Hey, it's our jurisdiction too," Rickenburg replied. "We ought to be doing the same."

Elijah sighed. "I guess that's why they have their own cops. God have mercy every time they need to transport a suspect to the County Jail. It's an hour drive one-way."

"Hey, it gives them something to do. A police department of a town of a hundred and seventy-something people. Mostly farmers who keep to themselves. Heh! I bet they spend most of their time roasting marshmallows in the woods."

"Not today, apparently," Elijah said.

"I think this is it here," Deputy Page radioed.

"Angel Drive," Elijah reminded him.

"I remember."

They followed the county interceptor to the right. After driving a mile down, they spotted red and blue flashers.

"Looks like we found their spotter," Page said.

They turned on their strobes, then pulled over to the side.

"Finally," Officer Harold Stan said to himself. The third-shifter barely had the chance to wake up when the call came in that he was being mandated to work early. He stood outside his vehicle, thumbs tucked underneath his belt while the other officers approached.

"Troopers Letson and McDermott," Elijah introduced. He pointed his thumb at the other two. "Rickenburg and Page with the County."

"Harold Stan."

"What's all the fuss about?" Rickenburg asked.

"I, uh, don't know exactly," Harold said.

Elijah groaned loudly, frustrated and tired, and somewhat cramped from the long drive.

"What do you mean 'you don't know'?"

"Dispatch reported that the Chief is missing. Now, the other guys fell off the grid. Nobody's answering their radios."

"So, why didn't you go in and check on 'em?" Page inquired.

"Because my instructions were to wait here for you guys. If you want to point fingers and ask questions, I could continue on with 'why did it take you an hour to even reply to our initial calls?'"

"Quit the bullshit," Elijah barked. Harold and the County Deputies stepped back from each other. "Looks like we have work to do. Can you take us to the crime scene, Harold?"

"Follow me. Be careful, these roads are shit to drive on."

"Last thing I want is a blown tire," Elijah said. He climbed back into his vehicle and glanced at the other officers. "Mount up. Follow the officer."

CHAPTER 23

With a Glock gripped tightly in one hand and Shane's hand gripped in the other, Christine ran south along the lakeshore toward the ranch. A wave of apprehension struck her when they arrived at the patch of woods where they originally encountered the beast. Despite this, she did not stop. She ran alongside her boyfriend, weaving between trees and other obstacles the forest provided. Her imagination went into overdrive, creating the illusion that one of these obstacles would come to life and snatch her up.

She was exhausted, both mentally and physically.

"Shane?" she said.

"Almost there," he said.

"Where is it?" she cried, looking over her shoulder for the beast.

"Don't look. Keep going. You've gotten this far. Just a little further."

He spoke the truth. After ten meters, they broke through the forest and emerged on the northside of the Beasley Ranch. Christine's chest ached as she ran along the west perimeter fence toward the house.

This impossible journey was reaching its close. Christine couldn't believe it: they might actually get out of here.

They ran past the barn and between the pens up to the house. By the time they reached the driveway in front of the house,

Christine's legs had given out. She spat and heaved, overwhelmed by fatigue and the mental strain of the whole evening.

Shane opened the driver's side door and leaned inside.

"Please tell me you actually can hotwire that," Christine said.

"Damn right I can," Shane replied. He knelt on the grass and removed the panel revealing the ignition wires.

As Shane began the process of hotwiring the truck, Christine couldn't help but watch the surrounding forest. Another breeze moved through the forest, as it had been doing all night, further taunting her with the looming threat that those trees concealed. Now, her imagination was making her hear footsteps. She could still smell smoldering flesh, smoke, and dirt. She would never be able to walk in the woods in peace again. This night had changed her. She wondered if she would even be able to sleep.

The truck engine came to life with a hefty rattle. It was an old and beat-up vehicle, but it worked. Shane was already in the driver's seat.

"Let's get out of here, babe," he said. Christine was already halfway there. She buckled herself in and gave the ranch its final goodbye. Shane flashed on the headlights and aimed the vehicle into the narrow driveway that cut between the trees.

He pierced the narrow pathway and drove around the bend. The trees were practically reaching down for the truck, like ghostly spirits trying to prevent their escape. Christine hated seeing the forest around them. Like when they ran through the forest on the northside, it felt as though the Bigfoot would emerge at any point. The sound of gravel being crunched didn't help.

Shane rolled his window down then slowed the truck. He stuck his head out to listen. That gravely sound was from tires—and not his.

Red and blue strobes stretched along the bend. Shane hit the brakes and turned on his brights to let the incoming cops know there was a vehicle in their path.

The first vehicle to arrive was Harold's Interceptor. Right behind it was a State Trooper Vehicle, and a Deputy Sheriff's vehicle behind it.

NOW they show up?!

Shane got out of the truck. Harold got out to greet him.

"Hey!" the midnight patroller said. "Where the hell have you guys been? Why haven't you been answering your radios? Where is everybody?"

"Get these vehicles turned around!" Shane said. "We need to get away from these woods. Hurry up!"

"Turn around?! What the hell happened?"

"There isn't time. I'll tell you when we get into town," Shane replied.

Christine stuck her head out from the window. "Harold, please get them turned around." Harold glanced frantically at the trees, then shrugged.

"It's too tight here. We'll have to drive up to the property to be able to turn around. You'll have to back up."

"Ugh! FINE! We need to hurry up."

State Trooper Elijah Letson stepped out from his Interceptor and quickly marched to the Oak Grove Police Sergeant.

"Whoa! Whoa! Whoa! Hold up for a sec," he said. "Let's put some context to this. Where's the Chief? You reported him missing. Where's the rest of your search party?" He shone his flashlight over Shane and Christine's uniforms. "Why the hell are you guys covered in dirt? And what are you doing with the civilian's truck?!"

"They're dead. All of them. It's just us left," Shane replied. *Goddamnit! Just turn the fuck around and I'll tell you later!*

Now, Trooper McDermott and the two Deputies had stepped out of their vehicles. Harold's jaw dropped.

"Dead?! Walter? Beau? Ed? Russ?"

"All of them," Shane replied.

"How many suspects are there?" Elijah asked.

"It's not human! There's something in the woods killing everyone. Now, we need to go now. It was chasing us, and could appear at any moment!"

"*Something?!* Like what? A bear?"

"No, not a bear."

"Then, WHAT?!" Deputy Page shouted from the back, losing his patience.

Shane squeezed his eyes shut. Would they believe him if he said Bigfoot? Probably not, but he couldn't think of a decent lie fast enough. Might as well give it a shot.

"There's...a humanoid creature in these woods," he said. "It's carnivorous and extremely violent. It massacred the entire Beasley Ranch."

"Humanoid? You mean Bigfoot?" Elijah said. He cocked his head back, his face threatening to form a grin.

"Yes!" Christine said.

The troopers and deputies exchanged glances. Shane could tell from their expressions that they were on the verge of laughter.

"It's not a joke! You think I would kid about my friends being dead?!"

"Dude, we have people on our department who say worse things about their *parents*!" Elijah said. "Besides, I don't know you. Now, we've driven for what feels like two fucking ice ages to get here. Back up and let us access the crime scene."

The sound of movement behind the trees drew Shane's attention to his right. Elijah backed up, hand cautiously resting over his weapon as the uneasy officer drew his Glock. It was pointed toward the woods, but as far as he was concerned, this guy had lost his mind.

"Sergeant..." he glanced at Harold, who whispered his name.

"Alter."

"Sergeant Alter," Elijah continued. "Do me a favor and holster that weapon of yours and..."

More movement followed, this time loud enough to get everyone else's attention. Rabbits and squirrels darted into the driveway, only to immediately disappear behind the trees on the opposite side. A few birds took off to the sky. The cops could hear something sizable moving its feet through the leaves.

Flashlights pointed into the trees.

"I saw something! Whatever it is, it's moving!" Deputy Rickenburg said. The others aimed their flashlights to where his was pointed. The creature was moving fast, then slowed as it neared the driveway. They saw brown fur hunched between two thick pines.

Shane wasted no time. He raced forward, aimed his Glock, and fired several shots into the trees.

"Holy SHIT!" Elijah exclaimed, backing away from the crazy small-town cop. A half-dozen shots rang out, forcing the others to draw their weapons. The creature raced forward, then collapsed at the edge of the tree line. The officers quickly converged on the creature.

Hooves raked the dirt as the dying moose drew its last breath.

Deputy Page took a deep breath, then glared at Shane.

"Nice one, genius. Is *that* what was hunting you? A damn moose?!"

Nobody was laughing this time, as Shane Alter still had his Glock pointed at the woods.

"It's out there. We need to move."

Elijah approached him. "No, son, I think it's time you hand me that firearm."

"Guys, he's right! We need to go!" Christine said.

"You too, darlin," Elijah said. "Hand over your weapons and the keys to that truck. Then we'll head back and figure out where to go from—"

A wall of branches exploded, the crashing sounds adjoined with an ear-shattering roar.

"HOLY CHRIST!" Elijah yelled.

The officers scattered as the nine-foot tall humanoid raced onto the driveway. Blood seeped from its burns and lacerations, and spit flew from its decayed jaw. It didn't bother sizing up the humans or strategizing the situation. It was on a rampage now.

Both fists crashed into the State Trooper vehicle, flipping it over as easily as a pancake. Metal and nature collided in a thunderous *boom*, resulting in a crunched engine and shattering glass.

Flashlights whipped all over the place, carried by frantically retreating officers. Gunshots rang out, sending projectiles zipping into the forest.

The Bigfoot glanced to its right and spotted the two deputies hurrying into their vehicle. They only managed to back it up three feet before its engine was caved in by two enormous fists. The

Bigfoot hammered the vehicle repeatedly, spilling engine oil, and ultimately turning the vehicle into a hunk of junk.

Next, it punched through the windshield. The clear panel burst into a hundred pieces of shrapnel that impaled the two officers inside. With glass hanging out from his face and hands, Page blindly reached for the door handle. By the time his fingers located the object, he smelled the stench of the creature's mighty hand reaching into the car. Next was the pressure of that hand closing over his right arm, followed by the sensation of being yanked through the busted windshield.

The creature held the deputy up to his face. Hot breath assaulted Page's nostrils, preceding a second wave which was carried by a deafening roar. Page screamed his last breath, which abruptly ceased as the beast extended its jaws, and closed them over his head. His skull imploded, spilling bone and brain into Bigfoot's mouth.

It spat the contents out then threw the headless body aside in favor of going after the next deputy, who had just stepped out of the car and was now running down the driveway. It only took a short sprint for the beast to close the distance.

Feeling its presence closing in on him, Rickenburg turned and pointed his Glock in a Hail Mary attempt at a lucky kill-shot. The shot went wide, the gun knocked from his grip. A whack to the chest knocked the Deputy on his back. Next came the intense pain of both shins splintering. The Bigfoot squeezed his legs in his grip, then lifted him halfway off the ground until only his shoulders were touching the dirt road.

Snarling, it pressed its heel to his chest, driving the breath from his lungs and crunching his chest plate in the process. That pain, however, dwarfed that of the separation of his spine. The beast hoisted his legs, while keeping his torso pressed to the dirt. His spine snapped and his flesh tore, spilling blood and organs as freely as a burst water balloon.

"Pop the trunk! Hurry up!" Elijah shouted to Alex, who climbed up over the driver's side door, now pointing skyward. He stood over it, then popped the trunk, allowing the Sergeant to access the M4 Carbine inside. He slammed a magazine into place, yanked back on the cocking lever, then spun a hundred-eighty-degrees to take aim at the approaching Bigfoot.

Several rounds punched through its midsection, spilling blood and fur. The beast howled in pain. These projectiles were stronger and more capable of cutting deeper into its muscular tissue. More shots hit its chest, causing it to dart back into the woods.

Elijah continued shooting in its general direction, even after losing sight of it. Meanwhile, Alex darted to the county vehicle, where he pulled out the high-powered rifle from its trunk.

"Guys! Hurry up! Get into the truck!" Shane shouted. The Troopers and Harold raced toward the vehicle and hopped into the bed.

"Go!" Elijah said.

Shane put it in reverse and sped back toward the ranch, while the officers in the back spotted for the beast. It was a gradual curve which was relatively easy to maneuver, so long as he didn't cut the wheel too hard.

Almost there…

Harold kept his flashlight on the road, which helped him navigate.

"Keep it going," Alex said.

They could see the property. Just a few more meters…

Branches exploded again, paving the way for a charging Bigfoot. Christine screamed as it connected with the truck, flipping it over onto its passenger side. The three officers in the bed were catapulted into the woods. Harold and Elijah summersaulted into the woods, while Alex faceplanted into a tree, smashing all of his front teeth.

Bigfoot peered into the driver's side window, immediately recognizing the dirt-caked uniform of the officer it had left to die in the pit. The bashing of the door shook the vehicle and the occupants inside. Christine screamed again as the beast tore the door free, then reached for her boyfriend.

Shane aimed his Glock at its head and fired. The sting to Bigfoot's skull resulted in the creature staggering back. It cupped both hands to its face where the bullet connected just over its left eye.

More gunshots echoed through the forest. Elijah fired in three-round bursts, striking the beast in its center-mass. Bigfoot lashed its arms at the air around it, as though trying to swat the incoming bullets to the side. Finally, it charged the Trooper, who raced back into the woods alongside Harold.

Alex McDermott rose to his feet, spitting blood and teeth. He felt the vibrations of drumming footsteps rapidly closing in on him. He pointed his rifle and fired from the hip. He only got off two shots before Bigfoot hammered a fist down on his head, crushing his skull down between his shoulder blades. The crunched, headless torso squirmed, the arms waving to the side like flags, before finally collapsing.

The beast could see the trooper with the larger weapon running toward the house. Its interest in the female had waned at the moment, as it saw the trooper as the greater threat.

The two officers reached the farmhouse's busted front door, which led to brief hesitation as they realized the building had already been attacked by the Bigfoot. However, the advancing threat left them with no alternatives. Both men rushed into the house and up the stairs.

Bigfoot burst through the entrance, widening it even further than it already was. It rushed to the stairway, only to be driven back by the stings of rifle fire.

"You like that?" Elijah spat at the beast. Angered, Bigfoot moved up the stairs, absorbing the bullets as it advanced toward its enemy. The stairway, already weakened from the initial attack on the Beasleys, buckled under the creature's weight. Bigfoot was almost within reach when the stairs fell from under it, dropping the creature to the floor.

More bullets struck its back, tearing into the muscular tissue beneath. Bigfoot wheezed, then spat out blood. Some of the bullets had torn into one of its lungs.

Elijah fired the last few rounds from his magazine, muttering "Fuck!" when it ran empty.

The beast stood and gazed up at him. The trooper launched the empty weapon at it like a tomahawk. The rifle bounced off Bigfoot's skull, angering it further.

"Trooper?" Harold muttered, grabbing Elijah by the shoulder and pulling him into the hallway. Right after, the creature leapt and grabbed the bottom frame of the hallway entrance. Like an athlete performing a chin-up, the creature hoisted itself onto the second floor.

"Oh shit…" Elijah muttered. He and Harold rushed into the nearest bedroom, which led to the realization that there was nowhere to go but out the window. The trooper dashed around the bed, opened the window, then kicked out the screen.

The house shook with each footstep. The creature burst into the room and roared at the humans. Elijah leaped to the patio below, landing on the grill, which toppled over with him. Harold jumped next, only for his fall to be halted after a couple of feet of distance. He felt the squeezing of his clothes resulting from the Bigfoot tightening its grip on his jacket.

"No! No! NOOOOO!" he screamed as he was hoisted back into the house. The beast rammed him into the wall, then rammed a fist into his face, pancaking his skull to the previously blue paint.

"Come on, just a little more," Shane said, pulling Christine out from the toppled truck. They looked to the house, noticing the subtle vibrations. The creature was walking back toward the front.

"What do we do?" she asked. She was looking at the truck. The engine was still running, but the driver's side tire was deflated. It was still capable of driving, but there was no chance of outrunning the beast for a quarter-mile.

"Help me flip it back," Shane said. They hurried to the top of the truck, then pushed as hard as they could. Slowly, the truck teetered back until gravity took over and dropped the vehicle back onto its tires. The engine sputtered, but still kept going.

A rolling crash echoed from within the house resulting from the beast dropping from the second floor back down to the living room. Shane started to aim his Glock, only to realize that would be a waste of time. He needed a larger projectile.

His eyes went to the truck.

A two-thousand pound projectile.

There was no time to consider the risks. It was now-or-never. He got into the truck and cut the wheel to the right, facing it toward the house.

"What are you doing?!" Christine shouted.

"You remember that propane tank over around the back?" Shane asked. Christine nodded. "Go get it. Hurry!"

Christine kissed him again, then sprinted around the back of the house, while Shane waited for the Bigfoot to emerge through the front entrance.

The beast stomped into the open, illuminated by the headlights. Its fur was covered in blood, its chest and shoulder red from third-degree burns. It saw Christine running around the side. It sneered, baring savage fangs.

Then, in the blink of an eye, all it could see was bright light.

With the flick of a lever, Shane activated the brights. Blinded, Bigfoot rose an arm over its eyes and stumbled backward into the house.

Shane floored the gas pedal and plowed the truck directly into the beast, bursting through the entrance and driving it back through the living room. The beast struck the backwall with a crunching impact and agonized squeal.

Pinned between the wall and the truck, the beast roared its fury. Immediately, it began battering the engine with its fists. Black smoke spewed into its face, driving it into a greater fury.

Shane rolled out from his seat and hurried around the back of the vehicle. The trap would only hold the beast for so long. He aimed his Glock at the fuel tank and fired until his mag ran empty. The smell of gas filled the room.

The Bigfoot pushed the truck backward, nearly driving it into its former operator. Shane jumped out of the way, struggling to get ahold of his cigarette lighter.

Christine arrived at the back of the house, where she saw Elijah on his hands and knees. Judging by his facial expression, he had probably cracked something on his way down.

"Get out of here," he said.

"No. Help me get this off," she said. She knelt over the grill and got the propane tank. Realizing what she was up to, Elijah helped her disconnect it then loosen the valve.

He tried to lift it, only for his fractured left leg to buckle.

"Let me," Christine said. She lifted the tank and hurried over to the side window. She could hear smashing inside from the Bigfoot's assault on the truck. With all of her might, she threw the cannister through the window, shattering the glass.

The tank hit the floor and rolled, spewing its propane gas into the living room.

Shane flicked his lighter, but the damn thing would not spark.

"Oh, come on!"

The beast shoved the truck further, fully freeing itself. It fell forward unexpectedly over the hood. Its hip throbbed, the impact having cracked a bone near the joint. The beast pushed up on its hands, then glared at the human again.

Shane had one more chance before it would leap at him.

He ran his thumb over the flint. Finally, a flame took form.

"See you in hell." He pressed the flame to the gas puddle under the truck, igniting a flaming river which streaked along the floor. He spun on his feet and sprinted for the front yard, clearing the building as the flame ignited the propane gas.

The house erupted into a ball of fire.

Shane continued into the front yard, then turned around to look at the inferno.

Christine and Elijah quickly joined him, the former limping on his left leg. They stood together and watched the ball of orange climb to the second floor. In moments, it had engulfed the roof and the east side of the building, where the kitchen was located. The fire burned through the gas lines, causing another explosion.

Deafening roars of a beast in agonizing pain filled the night sky. They could hear it thrashing about inside the building, blindly smashing walls, unable to find its way through the fire.

The orange glow was blinding, the heat incredibly intense, forcing the three officers to back up further. After several long moments, the crashing came to an end. The house was now an inferno. The smell of truck oil seeped from the flames, creating smoke that was as black as the night sky above.

The roars stopped. The terror had ceased.

Elijah collapsed to the ground, his mind numb from what had just occurred. He looked up at the two officers whom he had mocked just minutes earlier.

"My God. I never thought it was real."

"Nor did I," Shane replied. He wrapped an arm around Christine and watched the flames destroy his worst nightmare. It would go on to burn until morning, leaving nothing but scorched sidings, roof tiles, and bones.

CHAPTER 24

By morning, the Beasley property was teeming with State Troopers, Deputy Sheriffs, and Fire Department personnel. By three in the morning, the house had collapsed completely. By four in the morning, the fire department arrived, who proceeded to extinguish the already dwindling fire.

Shane and Christine watched the sunrise from the back of an ambulance. Officers were swarming over the ranch like ants, with several of them expressing confusion and shock after seeing the carnage in the pastures.

Droopy eyed, they watched the firefighters go through the debris. It had been a long night filled with seemingly nonstop debriefing by senior officers, who either couldn't, or refused, to believe what they reported. Sergeant Elijah Letson was somewhere in the crowd, probably giving his hundredth testimony on what occurred the previous night.

Christine leaned on Shane's shoulder. She was exhausted, but terrified of sleeping. She needed to see the creature's remains first. She NEEDED to know it was dead, otherwise her subconscious would haunt her for eternity.

"How much longer?" she asked.

"I can see the truck from here. What's left of it," Shane replied. "Any second now, they'll find it."

Christine looked up at him.

"I never asked how you were holding up."

Shane drew on a cigarette. He looked like he was deep in thought.

"You were saying something about moving. Going somewhere else with...less trees." He snickered. "I might've added that last part."

"I'm all for it," she said. "Maybe somewhere with water. Or open fields..."

"I like the water idea. Maybe find property along the coast," Shane added.

Christine looked at him. "You talk like you're thinking of involving me in these plans. Are they...long term?"

He leaned over and planted a kiss on her lips. She hugged him tight. She felt like she needed him more than ever. Nobody else would be able to get her through the trauma of what she had endured the previous night. No counselor, no friends, no family members, nobody at all.

Just a little more digging, and soon she would see its charred, hairless body. And everyone would know the truth.

"Nothing!" the Fire Captain called to them.

Christine's stomach ached. Her heart felt as though it was sinking into her gut.

"That's impossible!"

The Fire Captain slapped his hands to his legs, frustrated. "I'm telling you, we've been through this whole building. There's no body. No organic remains. Nothing!"

"That can't be right." Shane scooted off the ambulance and marched across the yard.

"I don't know what to tell ya," the Captain said. Shane and Christine moved past him and gazed at the wreckage. Much of the damage had been pushed aside from the pickup and loaded into dump trucks. They had expected to see skeletal remains lying nearby. Instead, nothing.

They stared past the foundation, noticing scattered wreckage that had spread past the patio.

"What happened there?" Shane said, pointing.

"You tell me," the Captain replied.

"That doesn't look like it was from the collapse."

"Probably not. Probably due to you ramming through the house in the pickup," the Captain replied.

"Not a chance," Shane said. He moved to the side, bumping the Captain with his shoulder as he followed the direction of the debris trail, which pointed toward the barn.

"Shane?" Christine muttered. She followed him. This couldn't be real. They would've seen it! It HAD to be buried somewhere in that wreckage.

There was a section of fence torn away which connected to the east side of the barn.

Was that damage already there?

Neither of them could remember.

They proceeded into the pasture and walked a few meters to the east. The water trough was turned over.

Shane absolutely remembered seeing that it was right side up during their investigation. He looked at Christine, and saw by her expression that she was thinking the same thing. They approached the huge puddle that had formed. Mud was everywhere. It was as though it had been lifted and spilled...as someone would do to extinguish a flame.

"Oh God," Christine said.

To the right of the puddle was a print leading into the grassy area, the remaining remnant of a trail gone cold. The print had already faded due to the dirt soaking up the water.

Smeared across that grass was a brownish red substance that had dried hours ago.

"No!" Christine was on the verge of tears. It couldn't be real. It just couldn't. She clung to Shane, who stared furiously at the dried blood in the grass.

The Blood of Bigfoot.

THE END

CHECK OUT OTHER GREAT CRYPTID NOVELS

BIGFOOT WAR
by Eric S. Brown

Now a feature film from Origin Releasing. For the first time ever, all three core books of the Bigfoot War series have been collected into a single tome of Sasquatch Apocalypse horror. Remastered and reedited this book chronicles the original war between man and beast from the initial battles in Babblecreek through the apocalypse to the wastelands of a dark future world where Sasquatch reigns supreme and mankind struggles to survive. If you think you've experienced Bigfoot Horror before, think again. Bigfoot War sets the bar for the genre and will leave you praying that you never have to go into the woods again.

CRYPTID ZOO
by Gerry Griffiths

As a child, rare and unusual animals, especially cryptid creatures, always fascinated Carter Wilde.

Now that he's an eccentric billionaire and runs the largest conglomerate of high-tech companies all over the world, he can finally achieve his wildest dream of building the most incredible theme park ever conceived on the planet...CRYPTID ZOO.

Even though there have been apparent problems with the project, Wilde still decides to send some of his marketing employees and their families on a forced vacation to assess the theme park in preparation for Opening Day.

Nick Wells and his family are some of those chosen and are about to embark on what will become the most terror-filled weekend of their lives—praying they survive.

STEP RIGHT UP AND GET YOUR FREE PASS...

TO CRYPTID ZOO

CHECK OUT OTHER GREAT CRYPTID NOVELS

RETURN TO DYATLOV PASS
by J.H. Moncrieff

In 1959, nine Russian students set off on a skiing expedition in the Ural Mountains. Their mutilated bodies were discovered weeks later. Their bizarre and unexplained deaths are one of the most enduring true mysteries of our time. Nearly sixty years later, podcast host Nat McPherson ventures into the same mountains with her team, determined to finally solve the mystery of the Dyatlov Pass incident. Her plans are thwarted on the first night, when two trackers from her group are brutally slaughtered. The team's guide, a superstitious man from a neighboring village, blames the killings on yetis, but no one believes him. As members of Nat's team die one by one, she must figure out if there's a murderer in their midst—or something even worse—before history repeats itself and her group becomes another casualty of the infamous Dead Mountain.

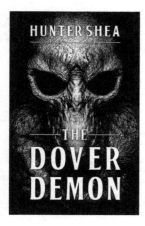

DOVER DEMON
by Hunter Shea

The Dover Demon is real...and it has returned. In 1977, Sam Brogna and his friends came upon a terrifying, alien creature on a deserted country road. What they witnessed was so bizarre, so chilling, they swore their silence. But their lives were changed forever. Decades later, the town of Dover has been hit by a massive blizzard. Sam's son, Nicky, is drawn to search for the infamous cryptid, only to disappear into the bowels of a secret underground lair. The Dover Demon is far deadlier than anyone could have believed. And there are many of them. Can Sam and his reunited friends rescue Nicky and battle a race of creatures so powerful, so sinister, that history itself has been shaped by their secretive presence?

CHECK OUT OTHER GREAT CRYPTID NOVELS

SWAMP MONSTER MASSACRE
by **Hunter Shea**

The swamp belongs to them. Humans are only prey. Deep in the overgrown swamps of Florida, where humans rarely dare to enter, lives a race of creatures long thought to be only the stuff of legend. They walk upright but are stronger, taller and more brutal than any man. And when a small boat of tourists, held captive by a fleeing criminal, accidentally kills one of the swamp dwellers' young, the creatures are filled with a terrifyingly human emotion—a merciless lust for vengeance that will paint the trees red with blood.

TERROR MOUNTAIN
by **Gerry Griffiths**

When Marcus Pike inherits his grandfather's farm and moves his family out to the country, he has no idea there's an unholy terror running rampant about the mountainous farming community. Sheriff Avery Anderson has seen the heinous carnage and the mutilated bodies. He's also seen the giant footprints left in the snow—Bigfoot tracks. Meanwhile, Cole Wagner, and his wife, Kate, are prospecting their gold claim farther up the valley, unaware of the impending dangers lurking in the woods as an early winter storm sets in. Soon the snowy countryside will run red with blood on TERROR MOUNTAIN.

CPSIA information can be obtained
at www.ICGtesting.com
Printed in the USA
LVHW052256291121
704802LV00033B/3112